Beach Pug

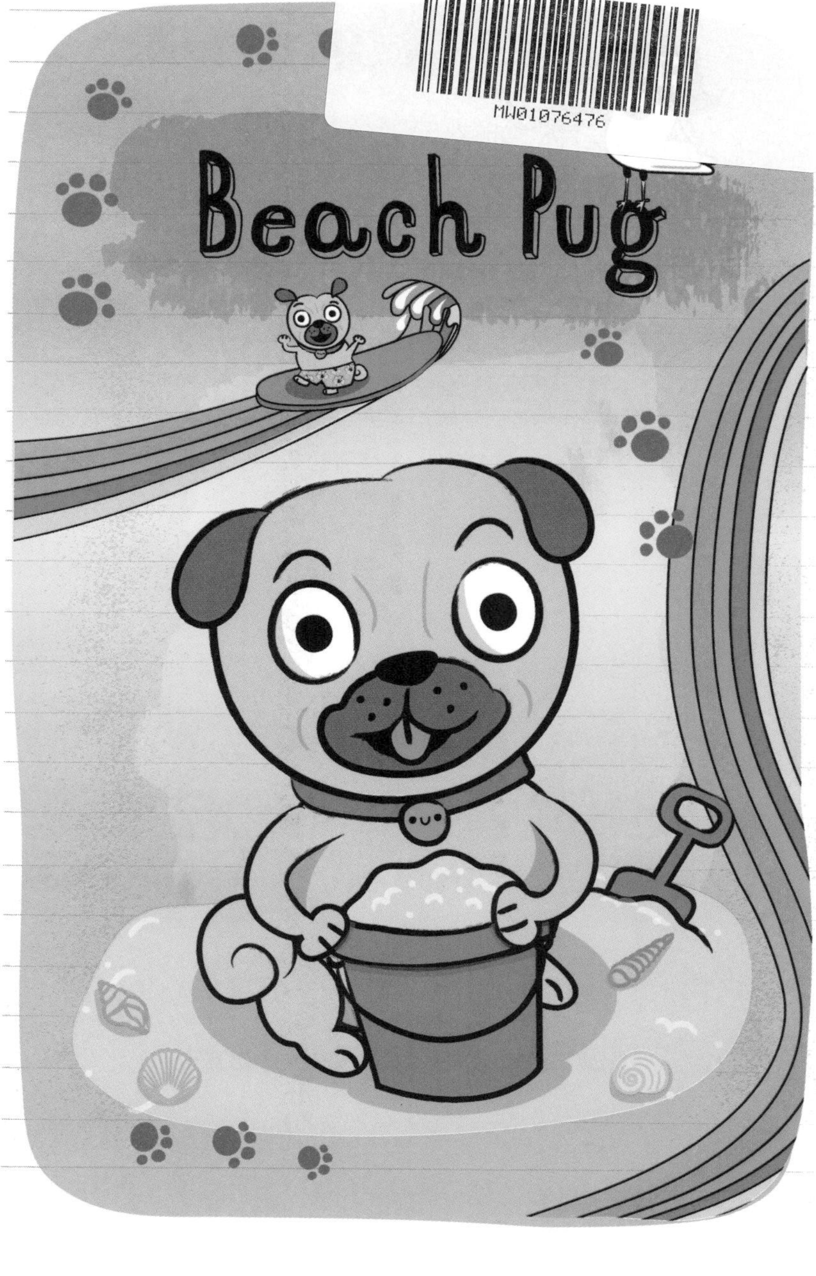

Read all the Diary of a Pug books!

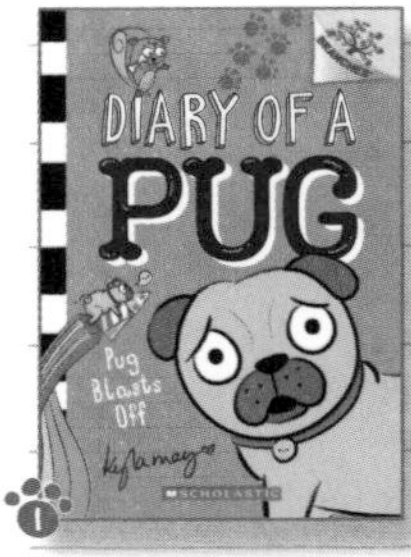
DIARY OF A
PUG
Pug Blasts Off
SCHOLASTIC
1

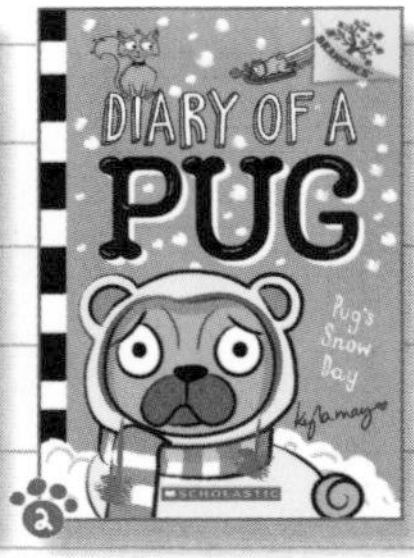
DIARY OF A
PUG
Pug's Snow Day
SCHOLASTIC
2

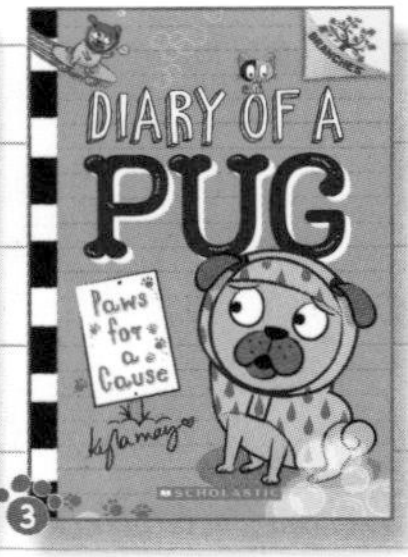
DIARY OF A
PUG
Paws for a Cause
SCHOLASTIC
3

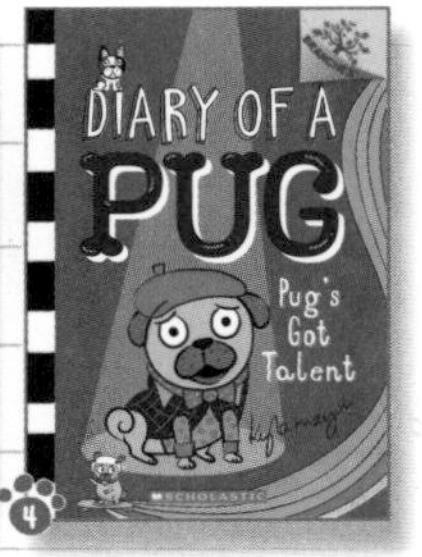
DIARY OF A
PUG
Pug's Got Talent
SCHOLASTIC
4

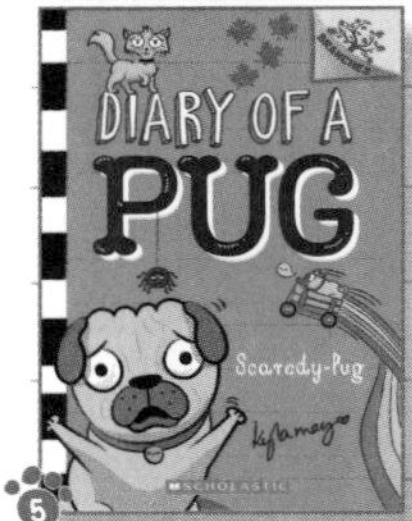
DIARY OF A
PUG
Scaredy-Pug
SCHOLASTIC
5

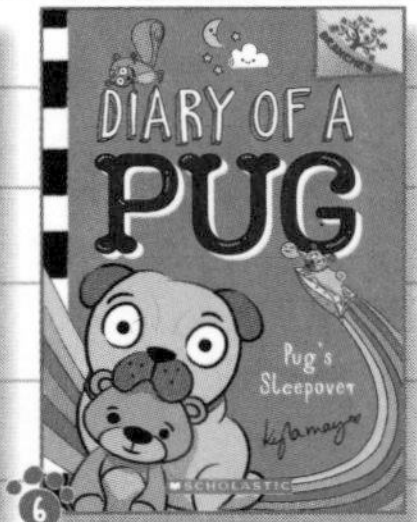
DIARY OF A
PUG
Pug's Sleepover
SCHOLASTIC
6

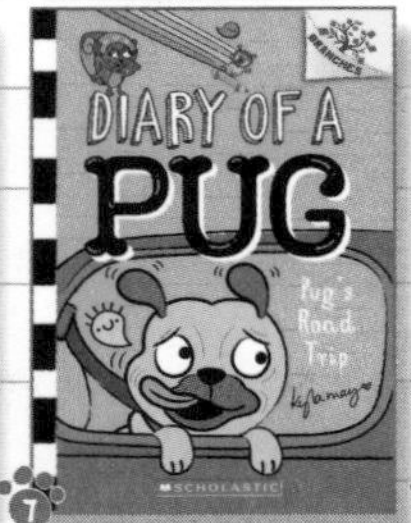
DIARY OF A
PUG
Pug's Road Trip
SCHOLASTIC
7

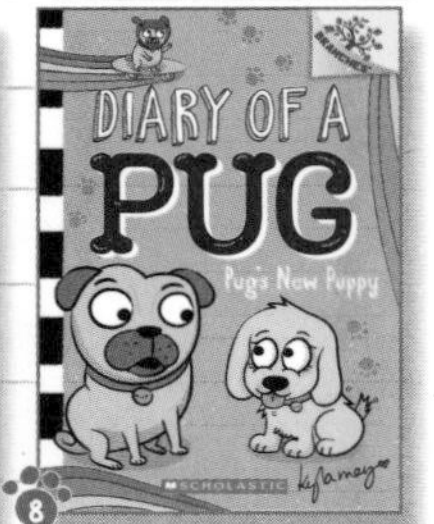
DIARY OF A
PUG
Pug's New Puppy
SCHOLASTIC
8

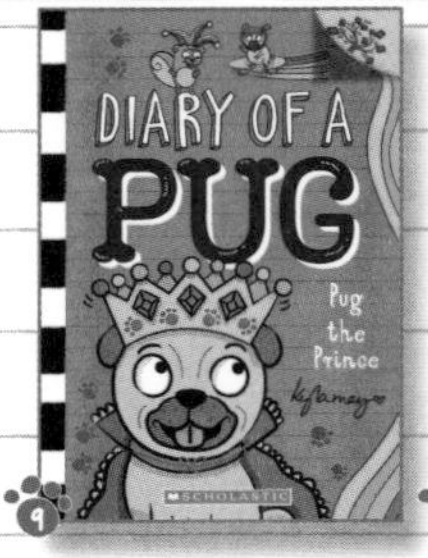
DIARY OF A
PUG
Pug the Prince
SCHOLASTIC
9

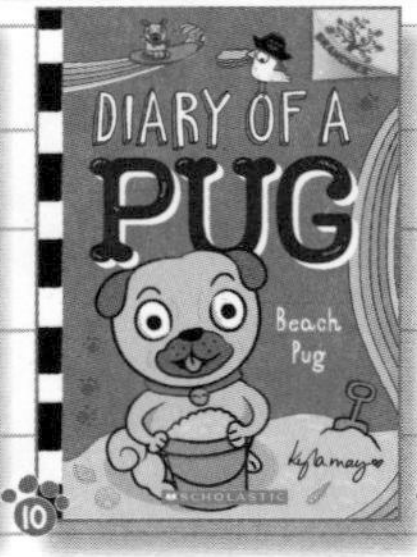
DIARY OF A
PUG
Beach Pug
SCHOLASTIC
10

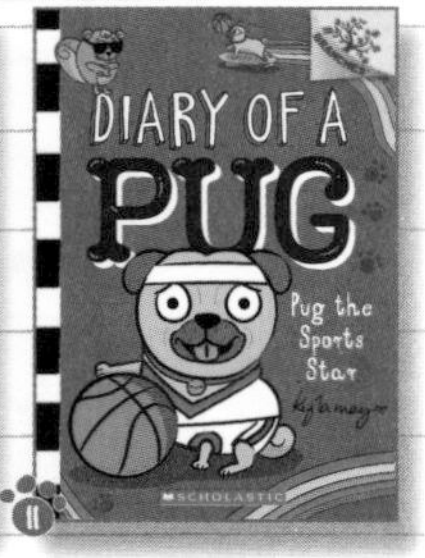
DIARY OF A
PUG
Pug the Sports Star
SCHOLASTIC
11

More books coming soon!

DIARY OF A PUG

PUG

Beach Pug

By Kyla May

BRANCHES
SCHOLASTIC INC.

I dedicate this book to my best friend Andy,
who loves the beach more than anything.

Special thanks to Meredith Rusu

Art copyright © 2024 by Kyla May
Text copyright © 2024 by Scholastic Inc.

Photos © KylaMay2019

All rights reserved. Published by Scholastic Inc., *Publishers since 1920*. SCHOLASTIC, BRANCHES, and associated logos are trademarks and/or registered trademarks of Scholastic Inc.

The publisher does not have any control over and does not assume any responsibility for author or third-party websites or their content.

Library of Congress Cataloging-in-Publication Data
Names: May, Kyla, author, illustrator.
Title: Beach pug / by Kyla May.
Description: First edition. | New York: Branches/Scholastic Inc., 2024
Series: Diary of a pug; book 10
Summary: It is Bub the pug's first trip to the beach, and Bella wants to enter him in a pet-surfing contest, but Bub is scared of the ocean and refuses, so he hopes to make it up to Bella by presenting her with the treasure at the end of the map he found.
Identifiers: LCCN 2022061968 (print) | ISBN 9781338877601 (paperback) |
ISBN 9781338877618 (library binding)
Subjects: LCSH: Pug—Juvenile fiction. | Surfing—Juvenile fiction. | Treasure troves—Juvenile fiction. | Human-animal relationships—Juvenile fiction. | Diaries—Juvenile fiction. | Humorous stories. | CYAC: Pug—Fiction. | Dogs—Fiction. | Surfing—Fiction. | Buried treasure—Fiction. | Human-animal relationships—Fiction. | Diaries—Fiction. | Humorous stories. | LCGFT: Humorous fiction. | Diary fiction.
Classification: LCC PZ7.M4535 Be 2024 (print) |
DDC 813.6 [Fic]—dc23/eng/20230117
LC record available at https://lccn.loc.gov/2022061968

978-1-338-87761-8 (reinforced library binding) / 978-1-338-87760-1 (paperback)

10 9 8 7 6 5 4 3 2 1   24 25 26 27 28

Printed in India 197
First edition, March 2024
Edited by AnnMarie Anderson
Book design by Kyla May and Christian Zelaya

Table of Contents

1. Bella's Beach Plan...............................1

2. Treasure Beach............................10

3. Beach Parties!............................20

4. Low-Tide Beach Surprise...............29

5. Beach You to the Boardwalk......38

6. The Best Beach Treasure...........48

7. A Brave Beach Idea.....................56

8. Bub the Beach Pug.......................65

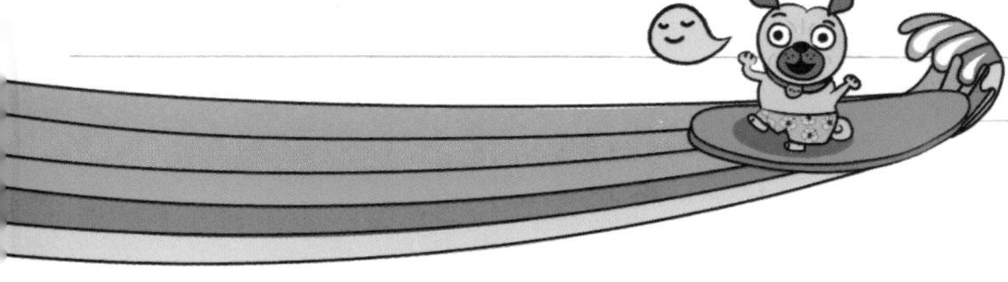

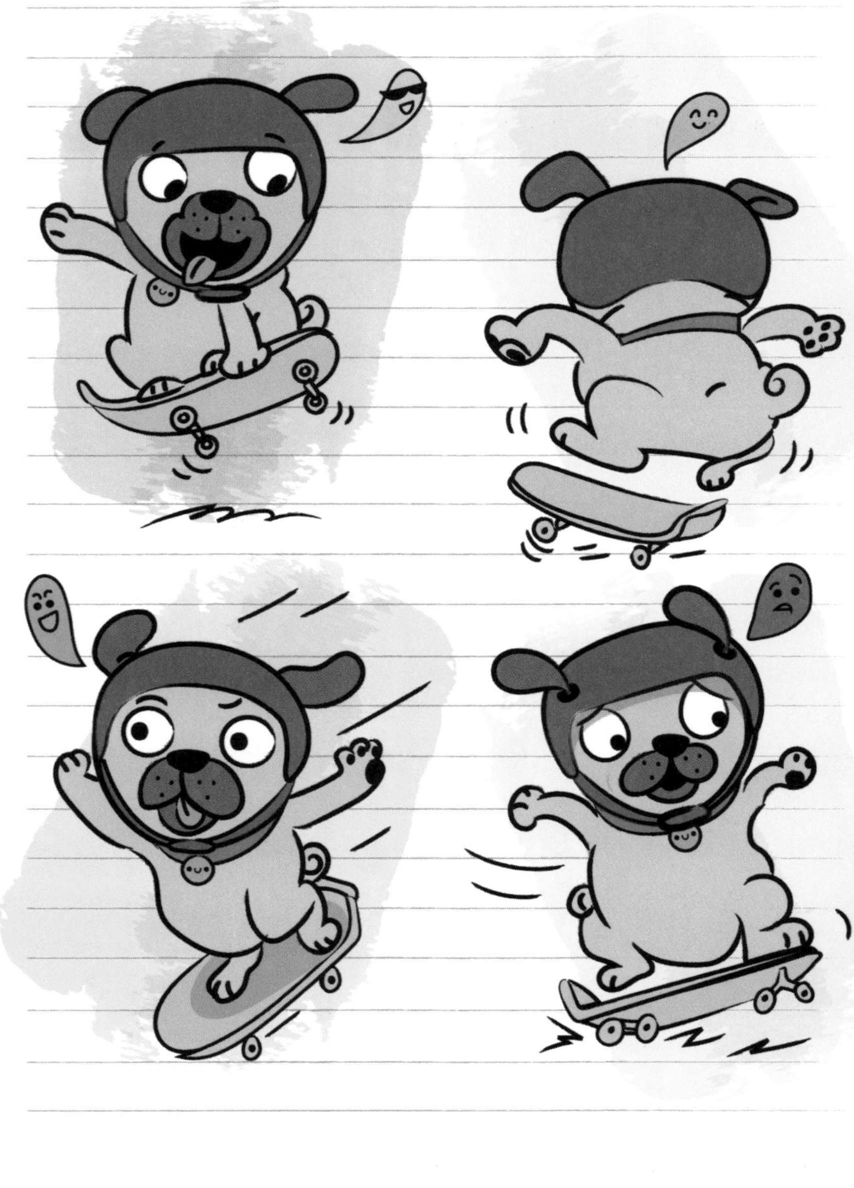

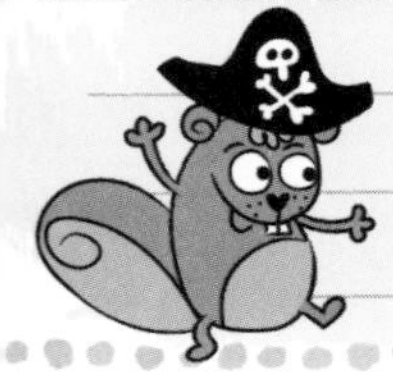

Chapter 1

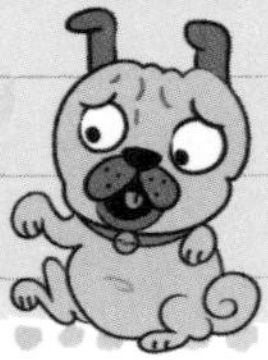

BELLA'S BEACH PLAN

MONDAY

Dear Diary,

Surf's up! Did you think you'd ever hear me say that? Me either! But Bella says I'm going to be a beach pug!

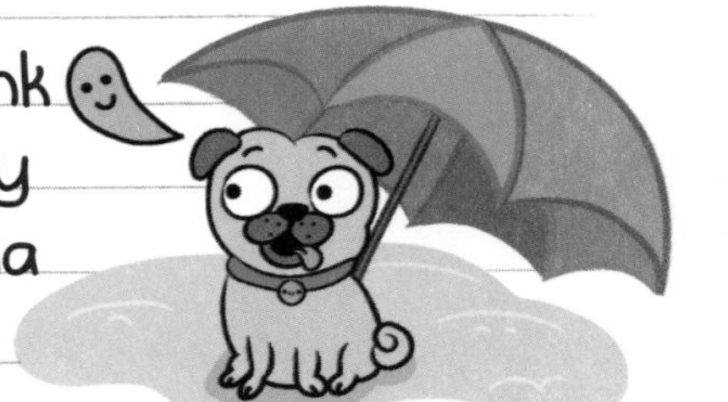

I'll fill you in on the details. But first, here are some things to know about me.

I've got serious skateboard moves.

I make many different faces:

Curious Face

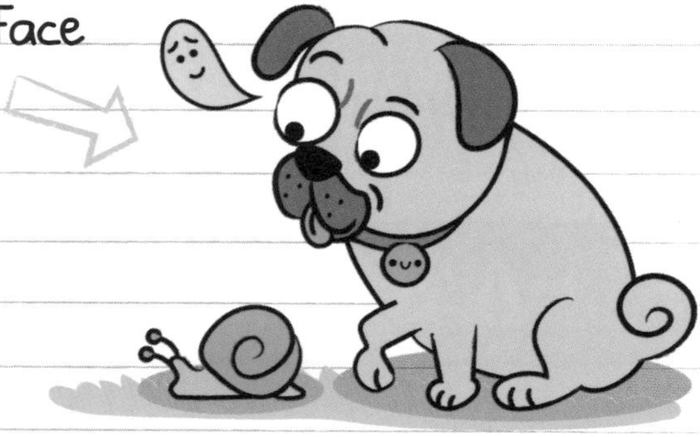

Let's Do This Face

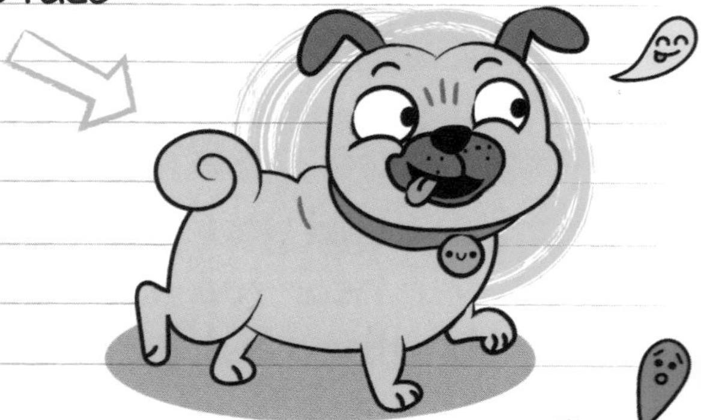

The Sprinklers Turned On Face

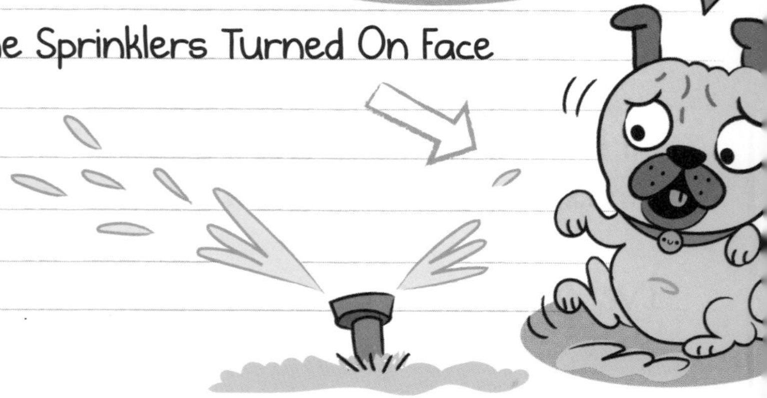

<u>These are some of my favorite things:</u>

MY BEST FRIEND, LUNA

PEANUT BUTTER EVERYTHING

DIGGING IN THE BACKYARD

Here are some things that get on my nerves:

DUCHESS

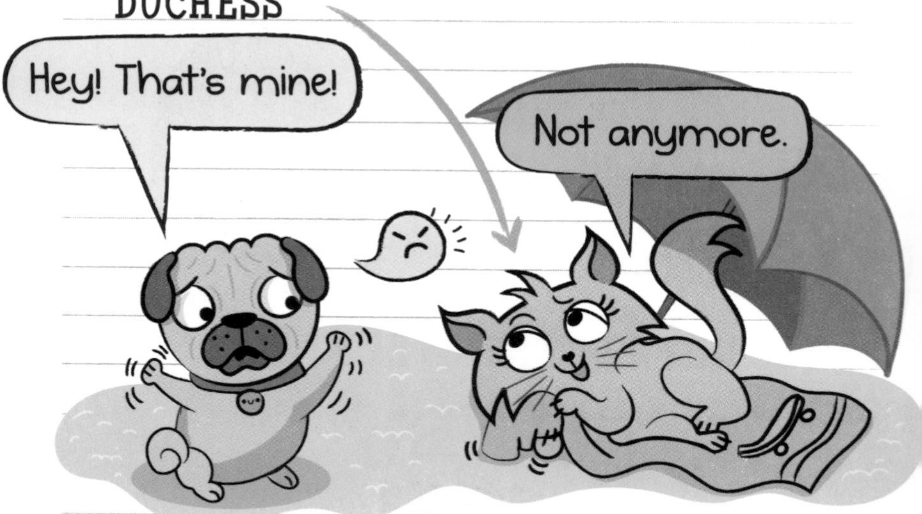
Hey! That's mine!
Not anymore.

NUTZ

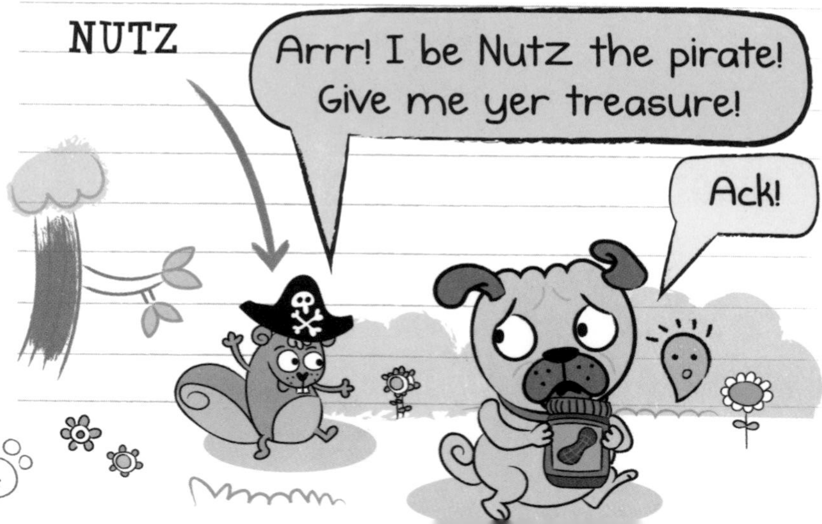
Arrr! I be Nutz the pirate! Give me yer treasure!
Ack!

And most of all, **WATER**.

I hate getting wet. Even. Just. A. Single. Drop. Which is funny, since water is how I got my full name: **BARON VON BUBBLES**. One time, Bella was taking a bubble bath, and I jumped in to play. No one told me there was WATER under the bubbles!

BELLA

Eeeekkk!

But back to the beach. It all started with Bella's big plan . . .

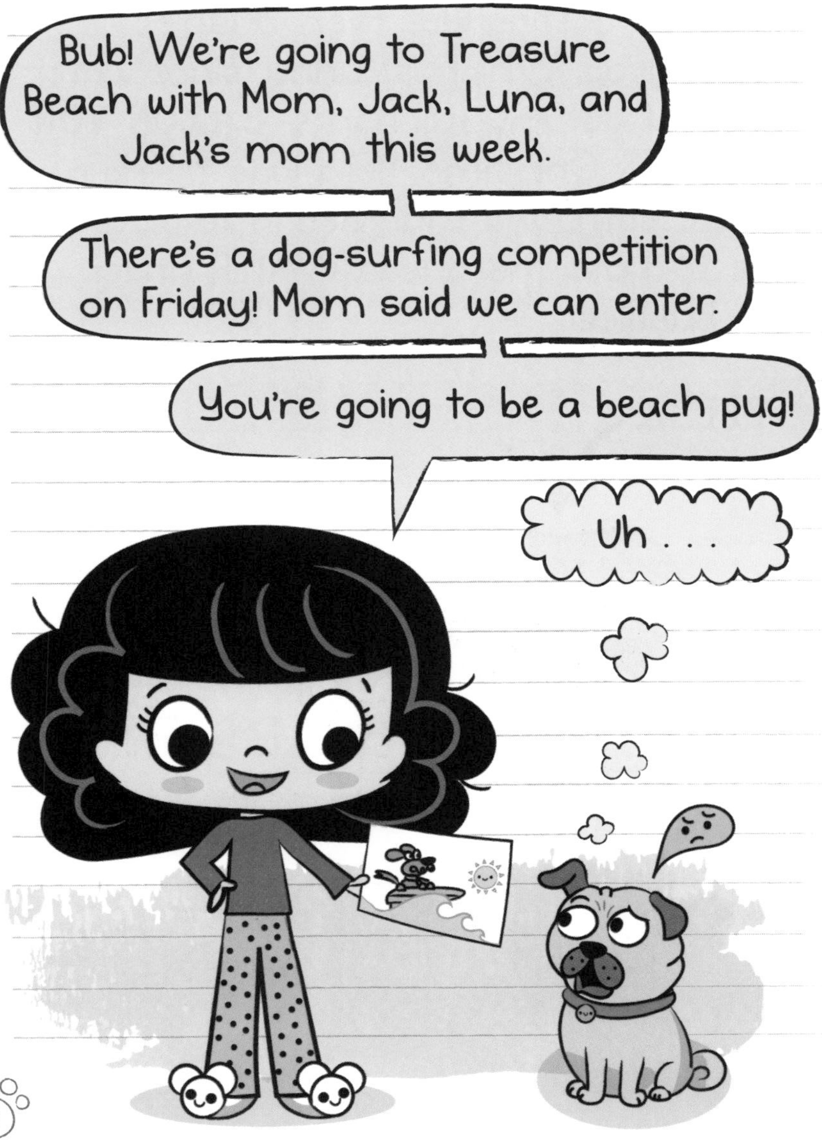
Bub! We're going to Treasure Beach with Mom, Jack, Luna, and Jack's mom this week.
There's a dog-surfing competition on Friday! Mom said we can enter.
You're going to be a beach pug!
Uh . . .

I've never been to the beach, Diary. But I've seen pictures. And there's one thing all beaches have in common: WATER.

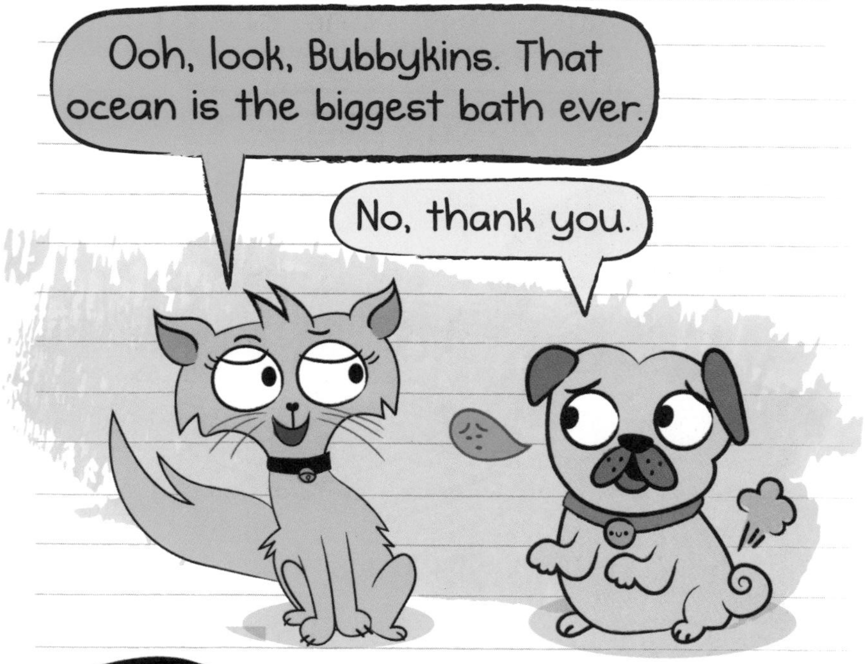
Ooh, look, Bubbykins. That ocean is the biggest bath ever.
No, thank you.

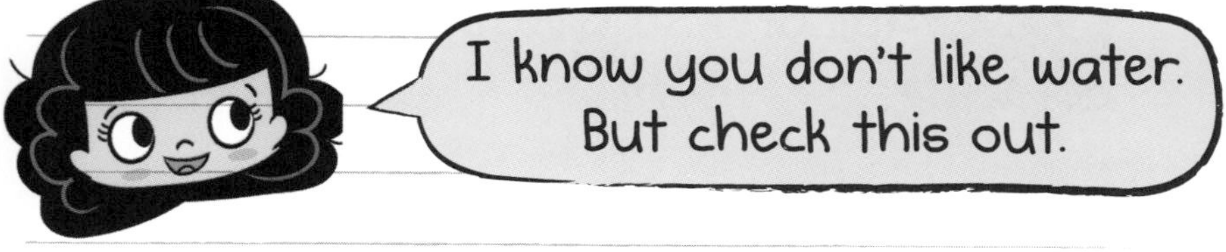
I know you don't like water. But check this out.

Bella could tell I was nervous. Because I toot when I'm nervous.

Bella showed me videos of dogs surfing. And I had to admit, they looked VERY cool.

Surfing is just like skateboarding, only on water.

You'll be a pro for sure!

Diary, I AM a superstar skateboarder. I never fall off! So maybe . . . I won't get wet?

None of the dogs in the videos were IN the water. Maybe I would be able to surf after all!

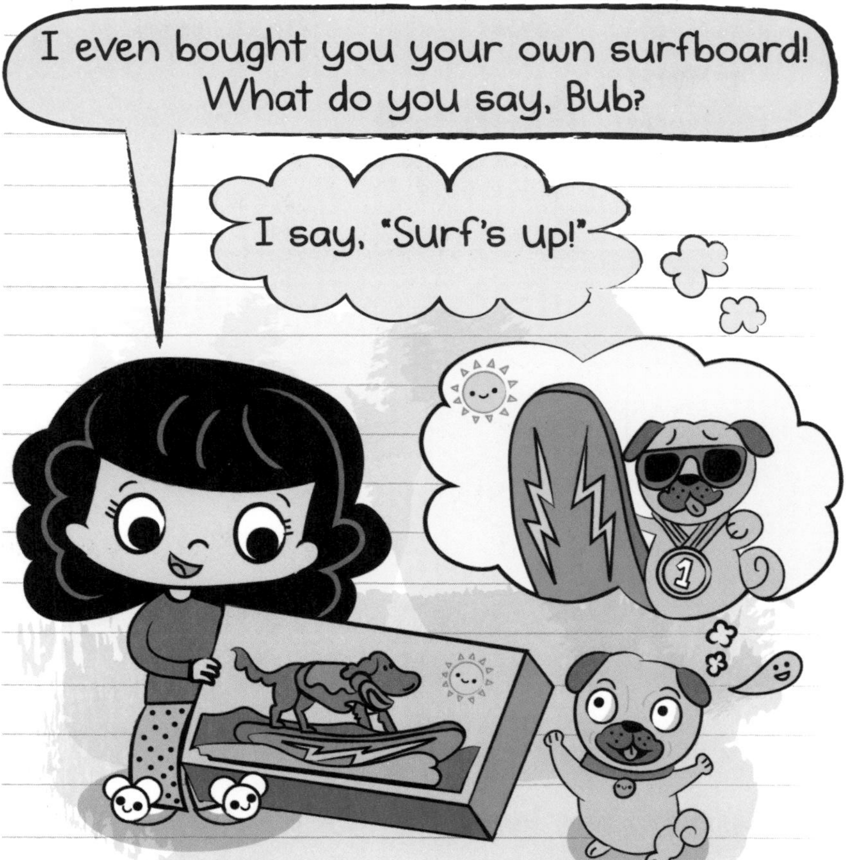
I even bought you your own surfboard! What do you say, Bub?
I say, "Surf's up!"

It looks like we're headed to the beach! Bella's mom will drive us tomorrow morning. Diary, do you think I can win a surfing competition?

Chapter 2

TREASURE BEACH

TUESDAY

Dear Diary,

Today we reached Treasure Beach. And here's what I learned:

1) Beaches are hot.
2) Beaches are sunny.
3) Beaches have SO MUCH SAND!

I could dig here forever!

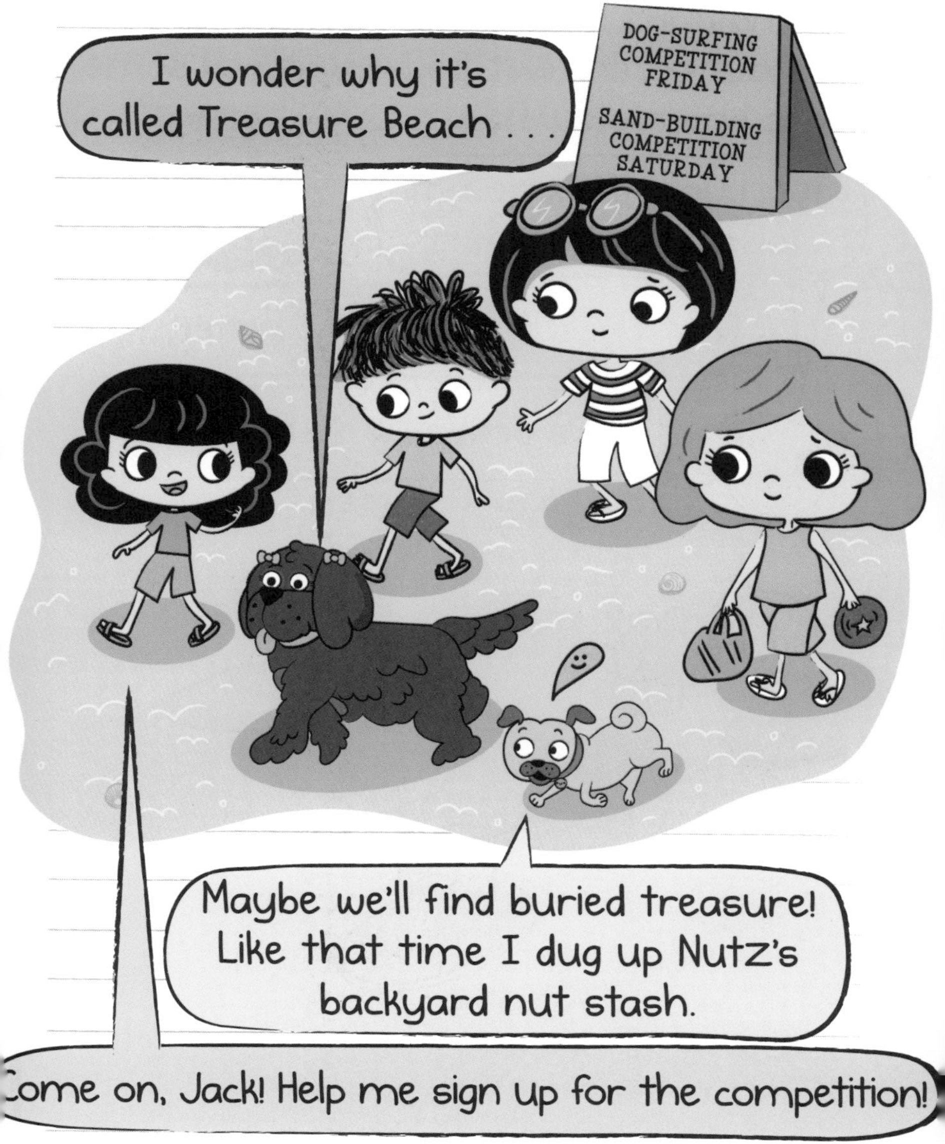
I wonder why it's called Treasure Beach . . .
DOG-SURFING COMPETITION FRIDAY
SAND-BUILDING COMPETITION SATURDAY
Maybe we'll find buried treasure! Like that time I dug up NutZ's backyard nut stash.
Come on, Jack! Help me sign up for the competition!

Luna didn't believe me that I could surf without getting wet. So we watched some dogs practice surfing.

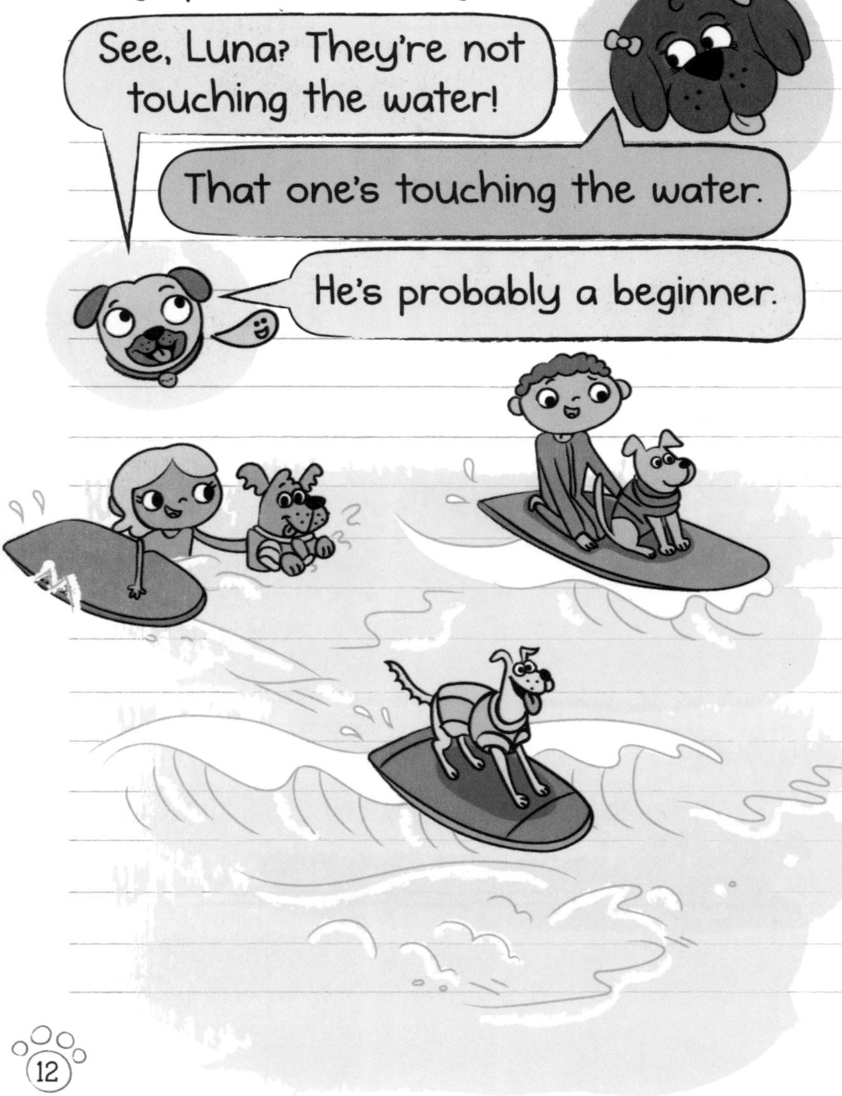
See, Luna? They're not touching the water!
That one's touching the water.
He's probably a beginner.

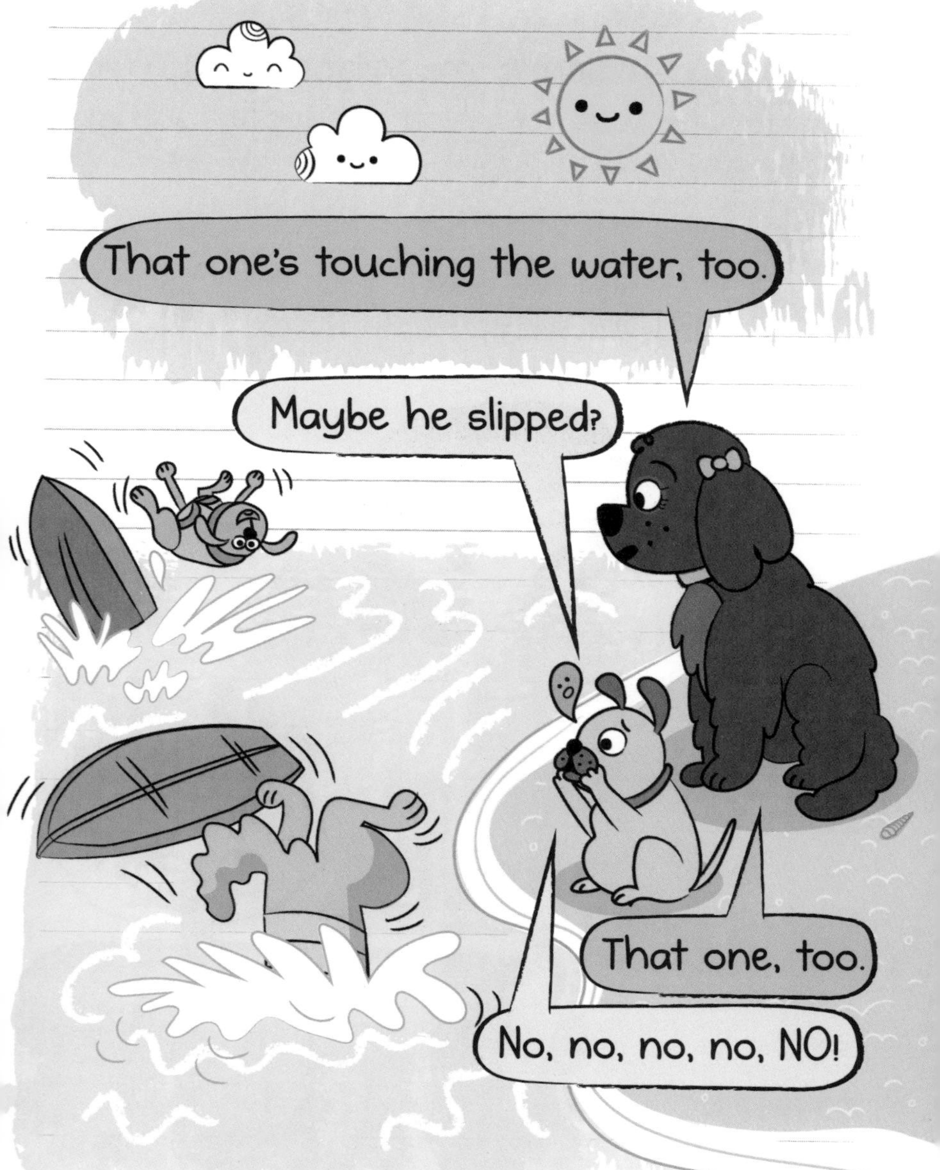
That one's touching the water, too.
Maybe he slipped?
That one, too.
No, no, no, no, NO!

This was NOT like the videos at all! EVERYONE was touching the water! When Bella got back, I had to let her know!

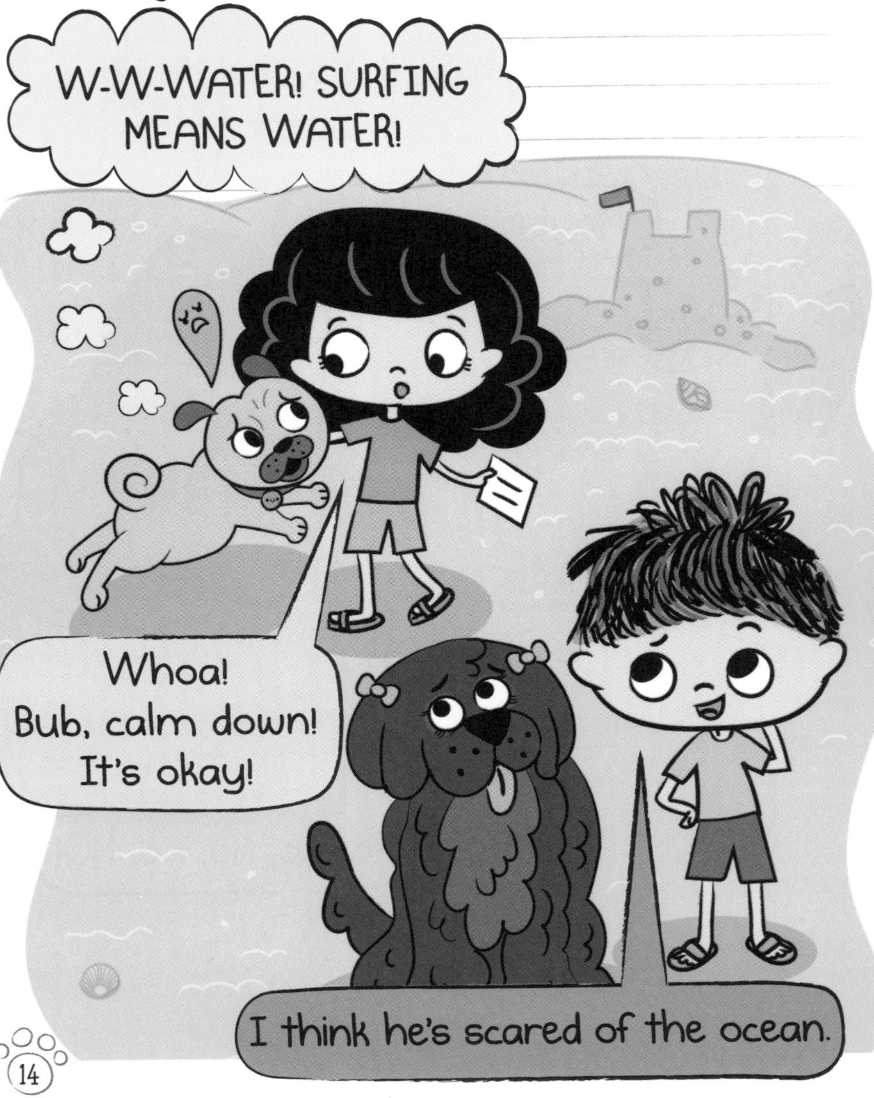
W-W-WATER! SURFING MEANS WATER!
Whoa! Bub, calm down! It's okay!
I think he's scared of the ocean.

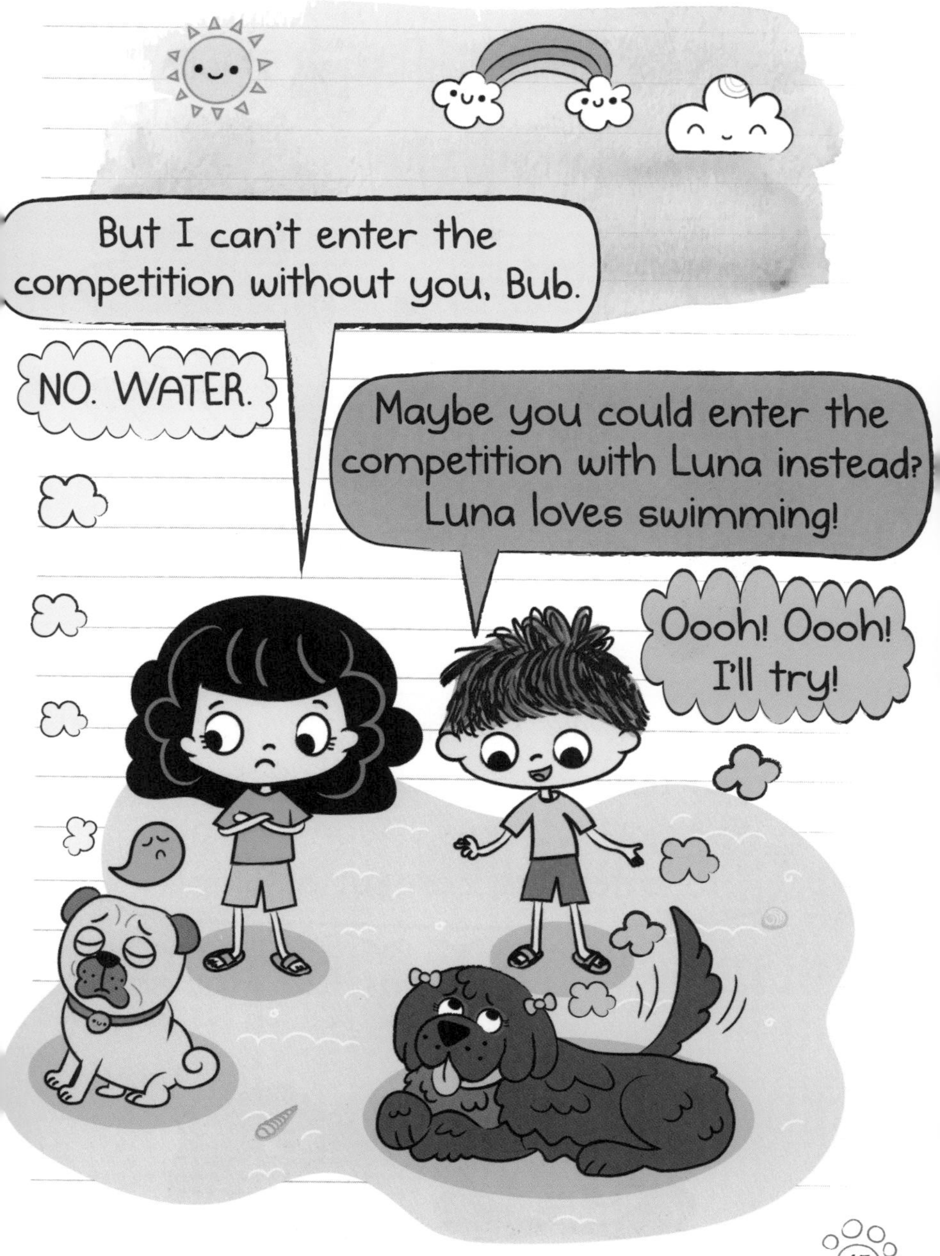
But I can't enter the competition without you, Bub.
NO. WATER.
Maybe you could enter the competition with Luna instead? Luna loves swimming!
Oooh! Oooh! I'll try!

Bella tried surfing with Luna. It was very . . . wet.

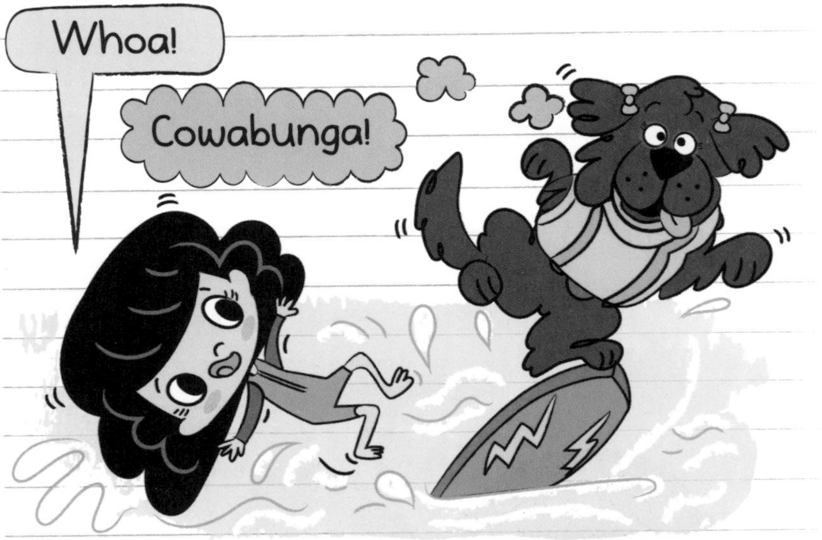
Whoa!
Cowabunga!

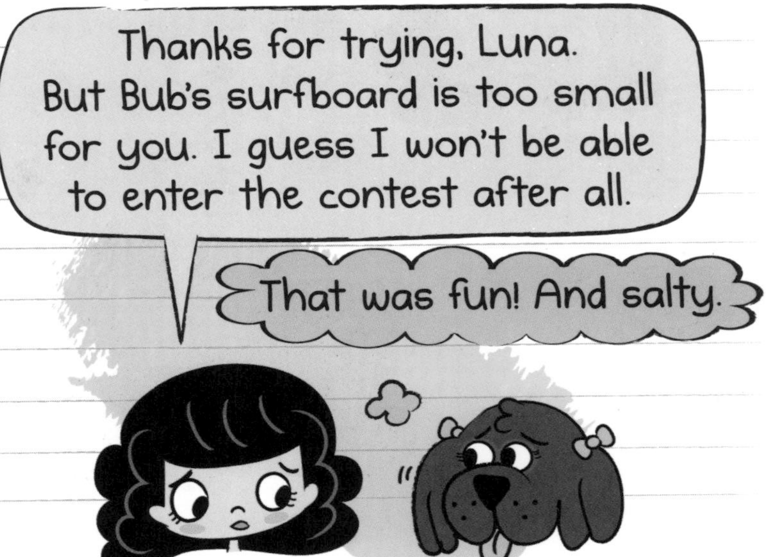
Thanks for trying, Luna. But Bub's surfboard is too small for you. I guess I won't be able to enter the contest after all.
That was fun! And salty.

I felt bad about letting Bella down, Diary.

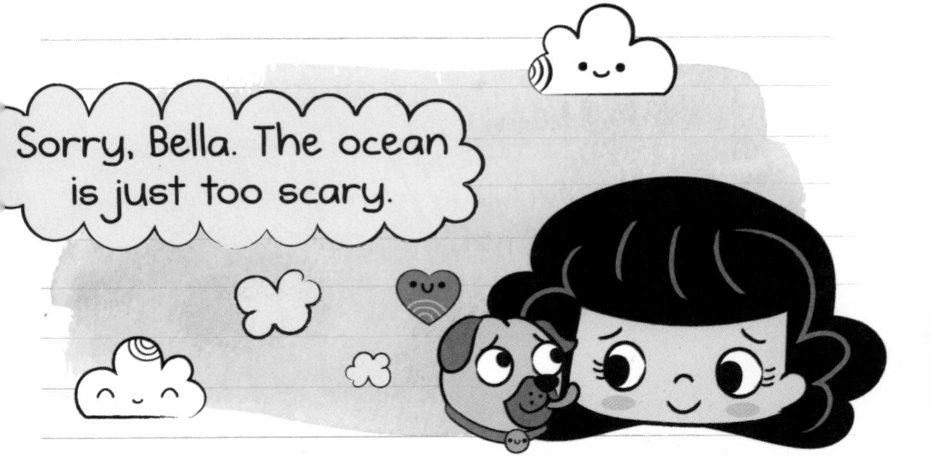
Sorry, Bella. The ocean is just too scary.

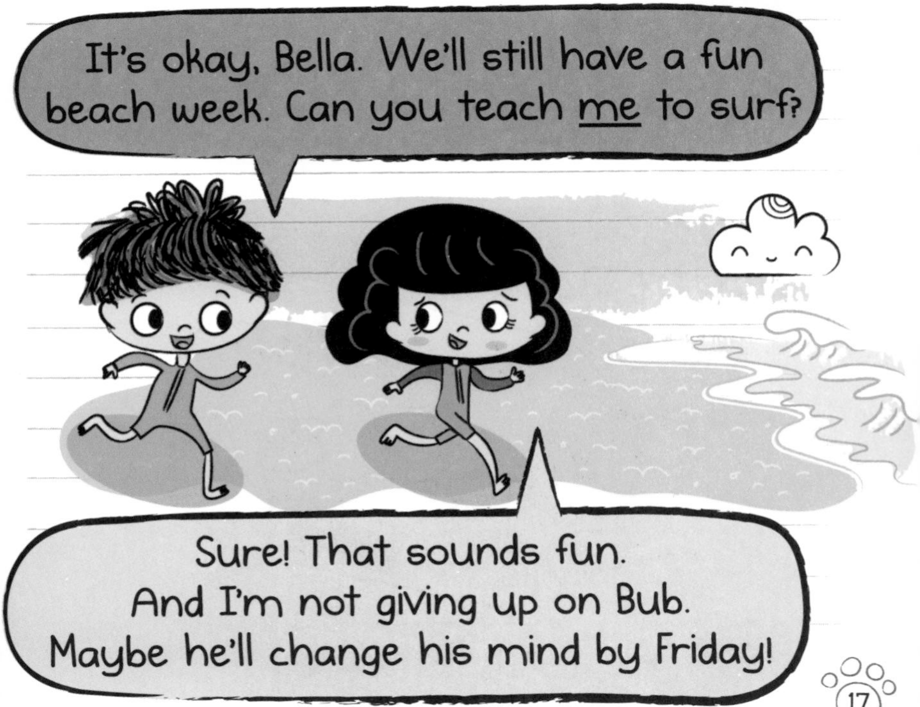
It's okay, Bella. We'll still have a fun beach week. Can you teach me to surf?
Sure! That sounds fun. And I'm not giving up on Bub. Maybe he'll change his mind by Friday!

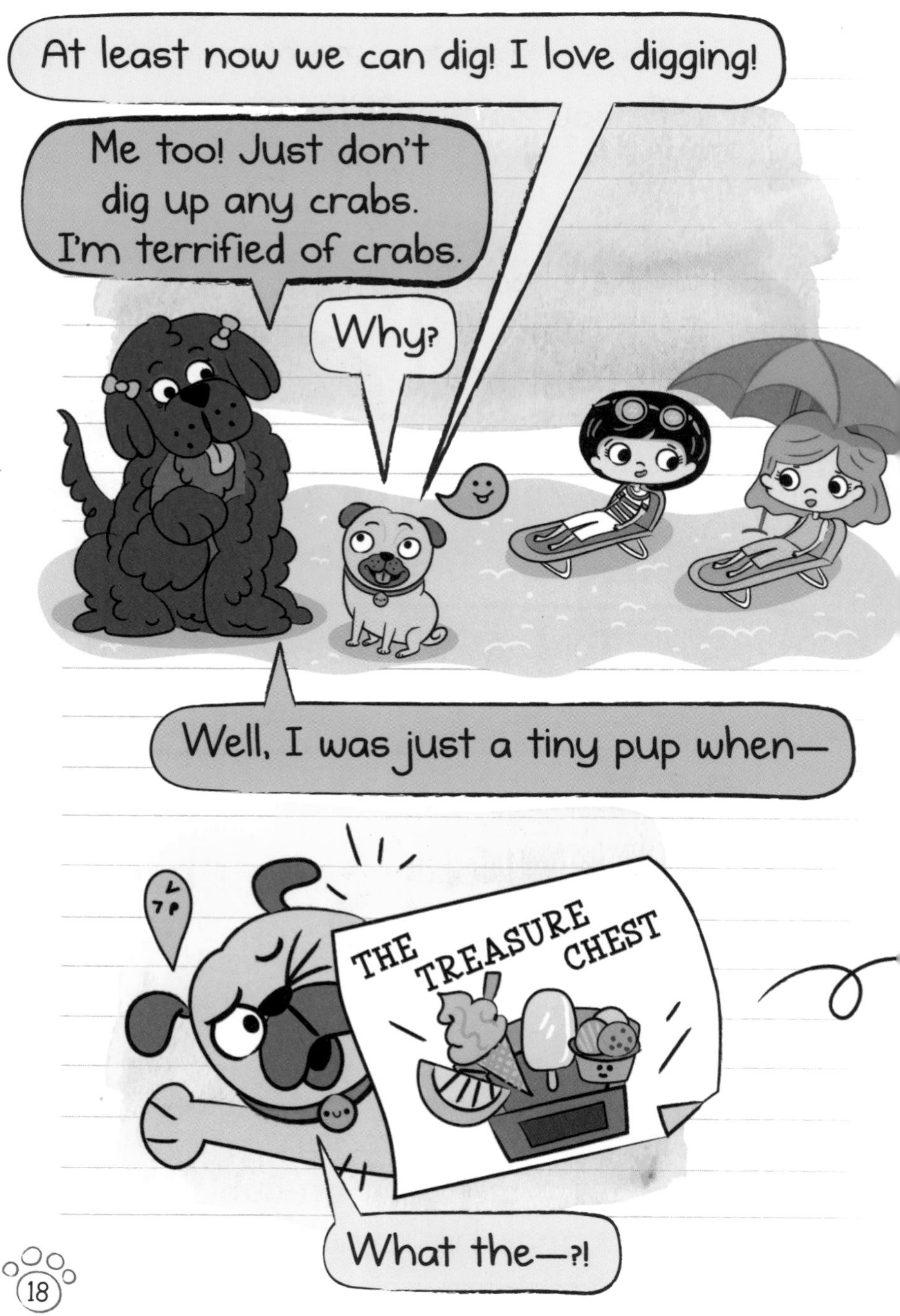
At least now we can dig! I love digging!
Me too! Just don't dig up any crabs. I'm terrified of crabs.
Why?
Well, I was just a tiny pup when—
THE TREASURE CHEST
What the—?!

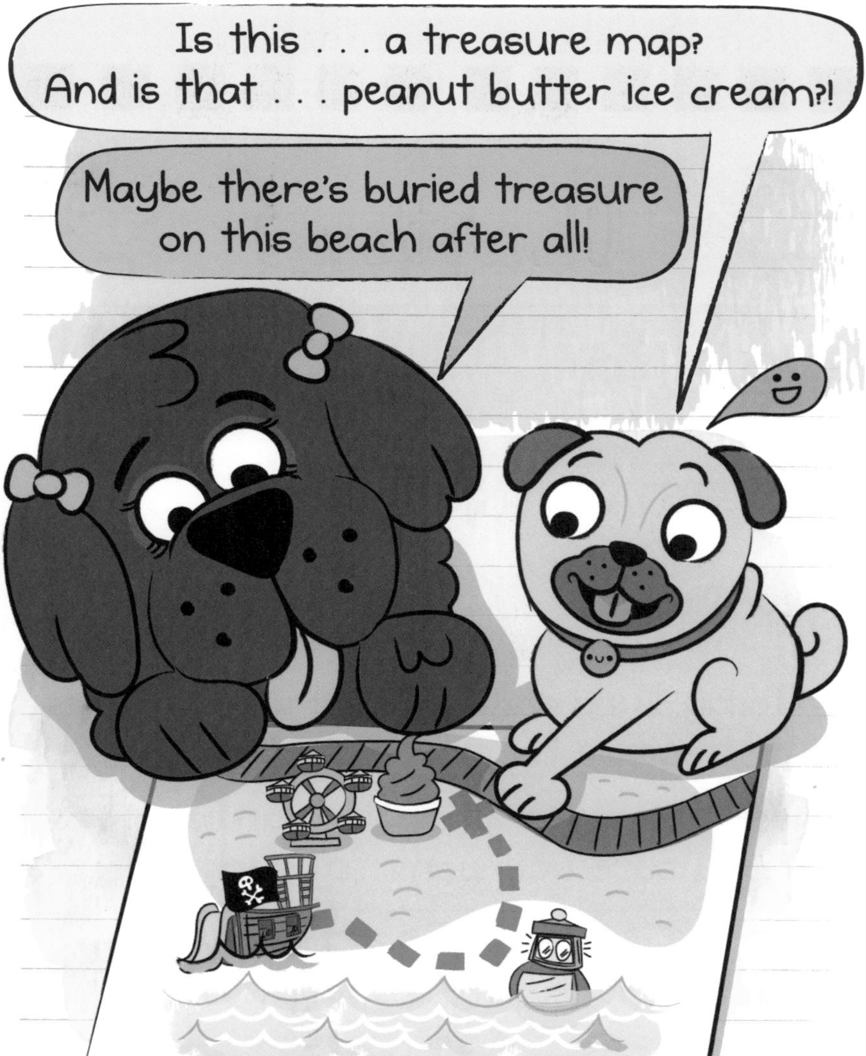
Is this . . . a treasure map?
And is that . . . peanut butter ice cream?!
Maybe there's buried treasure
on this beach after all!

Could there really be peanut butter treasure hidden at Treasure Beach? We're going on a treasure hunt!

Chapter 3

BEACH PARTIES!

WEDNESDAY

Dear Diary,

Today, Luna and I couldn't wait to go on our treasure hunt!

I made you a peanut butter sandwich! Are you sure you won't try surfing?

Sandwich, yay! Surfing, no, thanks.

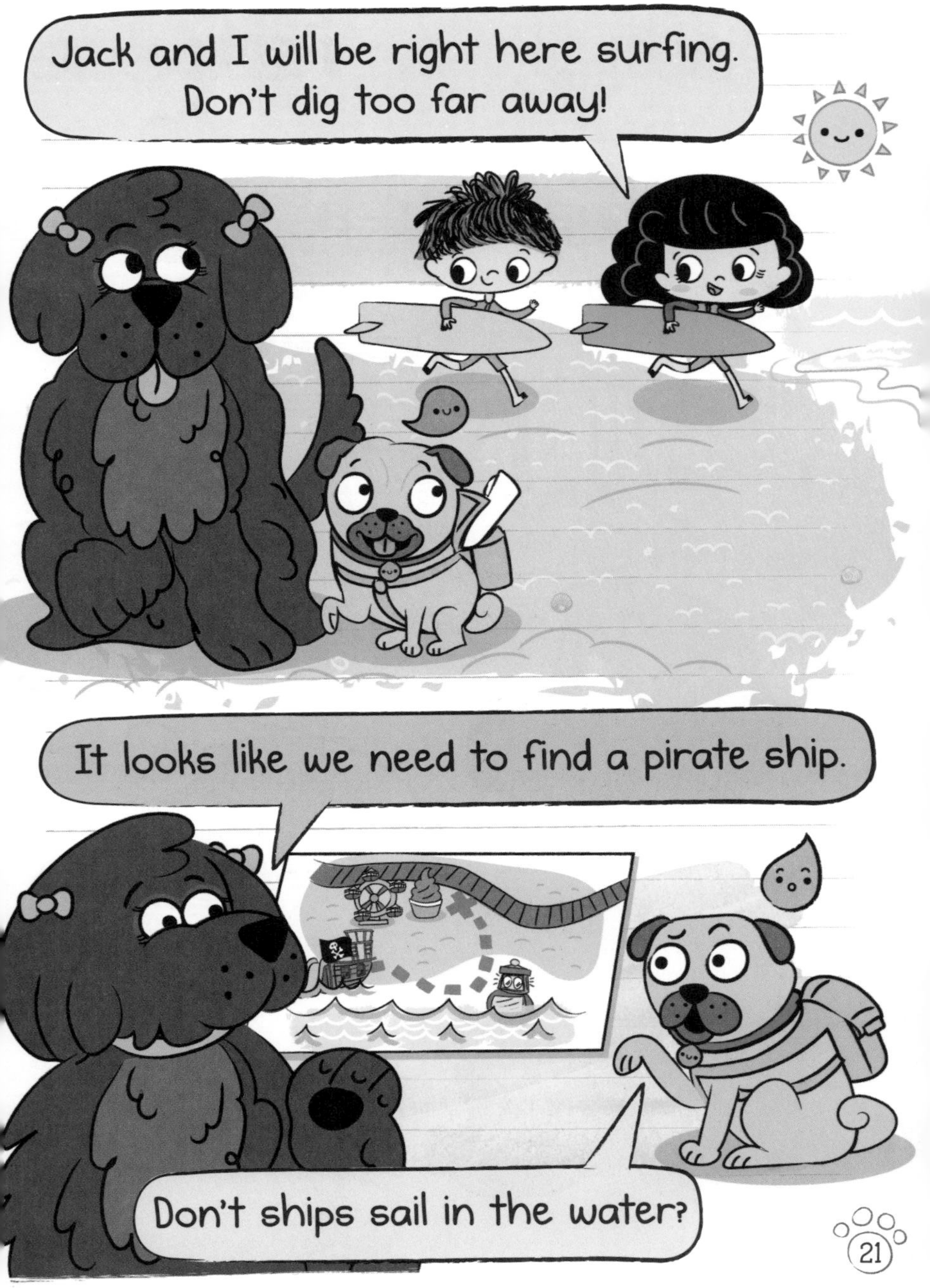
Jack and I will be right here surfing. Don't dig too far away!
It looks like we need to find a pirate ship.
Don't ships sail in the water?

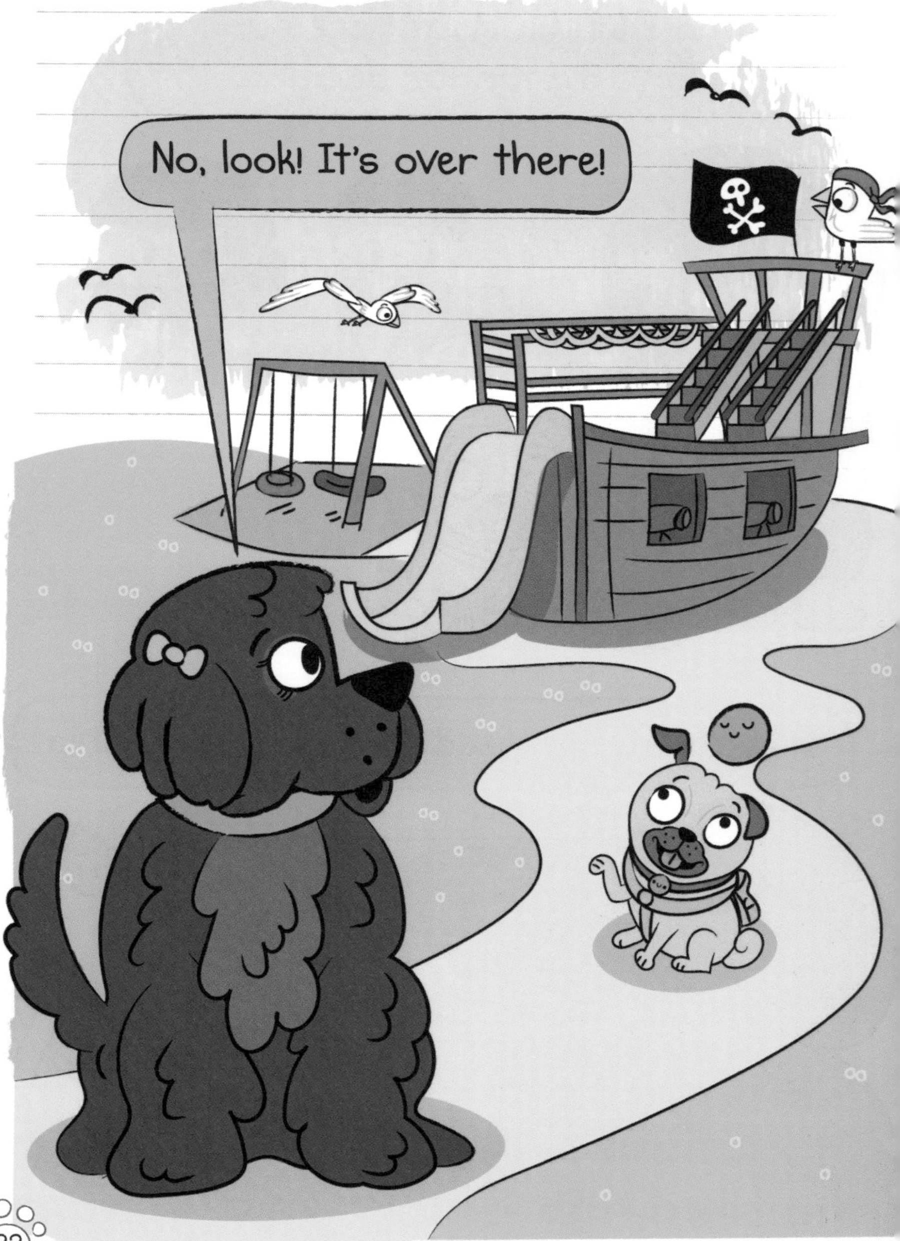
No, look! It's over there!

Luna and I found the first stop on the map! But the ship was covered in pirate seagulls.

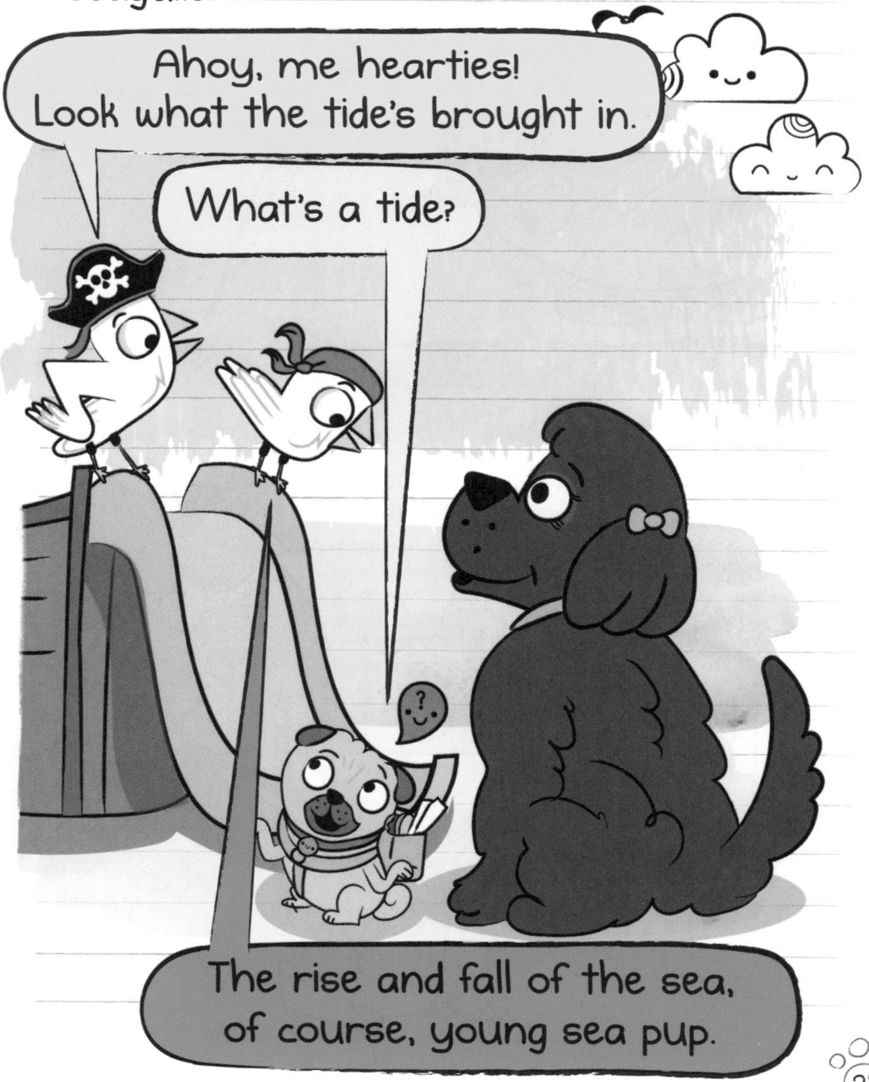
Ahoy, me hearties! Look what the tide's brought in.
What's a tide?
?
The rise and fall of the sea, of course, young sea pup.

Be ye searching for the long-lost treasure of peanut butter?
Eeek! You saw our map!
Few make it to the second spot on the map . . . the lighthouse in the ocean.
It's in the ocean?!

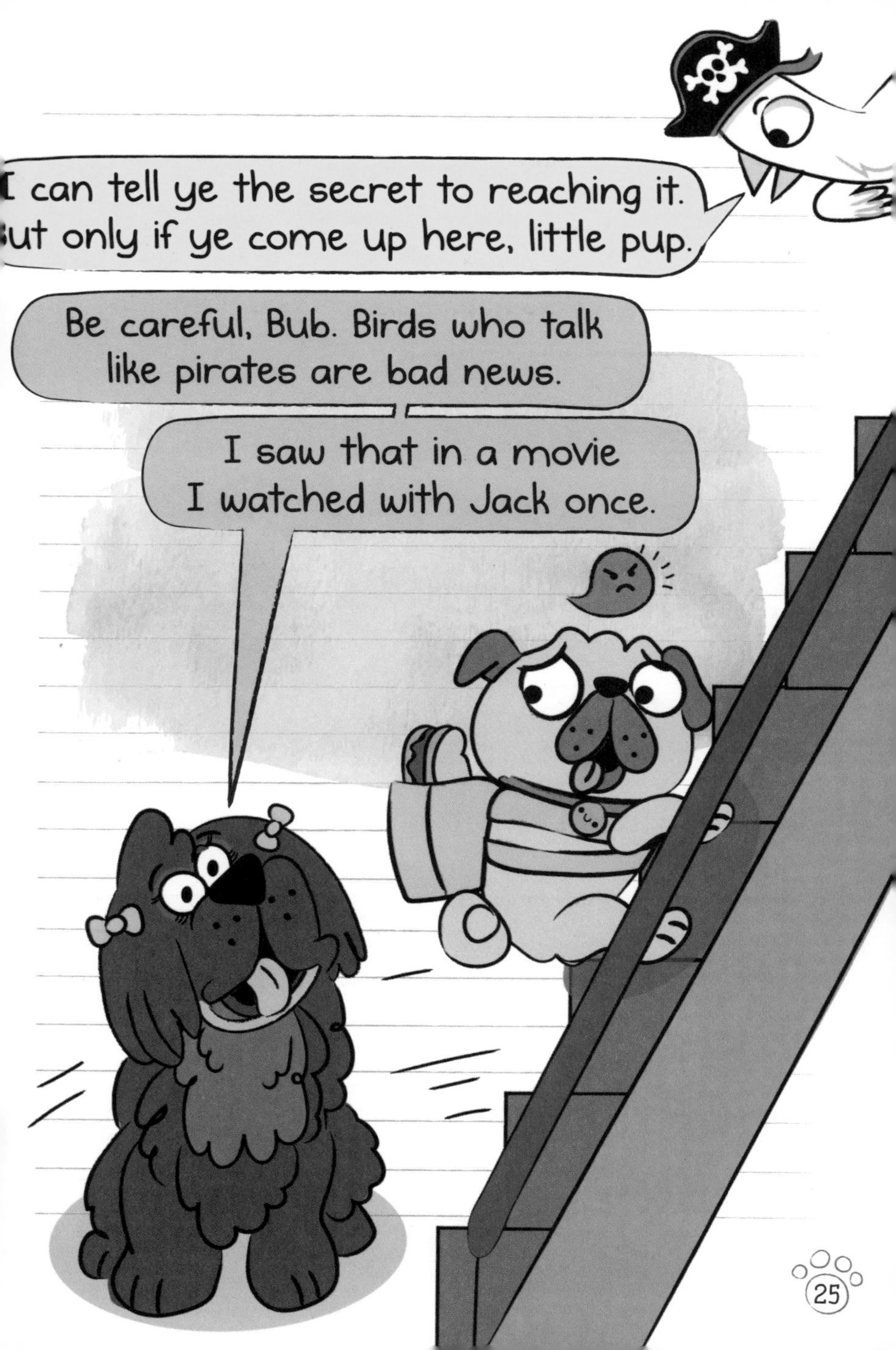
I can tell ye the secret to reaching it.
ut only if ye come up here, little pup.
Be careful, Bub. Birds who talk like pirates are bad news.
I saw that in a movie I watched with Jack once.

I could see far from up high. The pirate seagull pointed to the lighthouse.

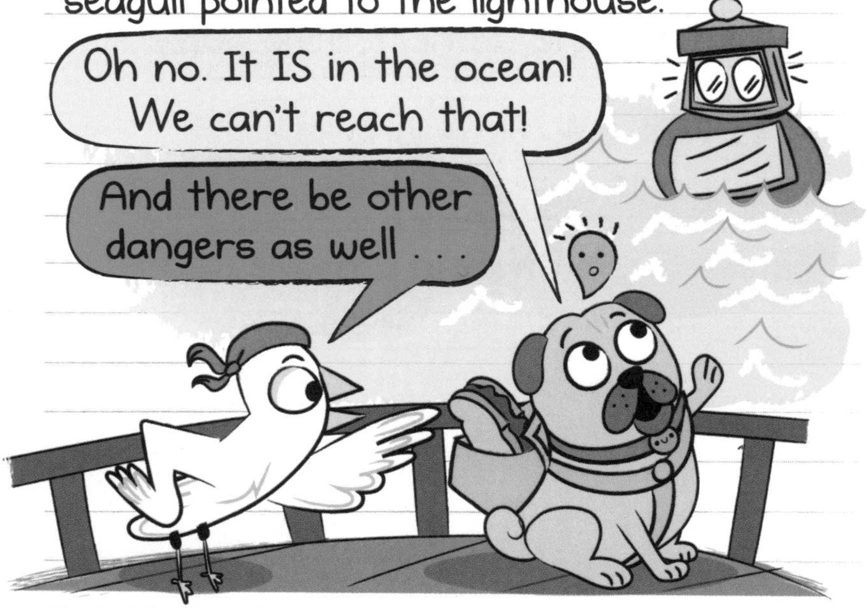
Oh no. It IS in the ocean! We can't reach that!
And there be other dangers as well . . .

Luna was right—the seagulls WERE bad news!

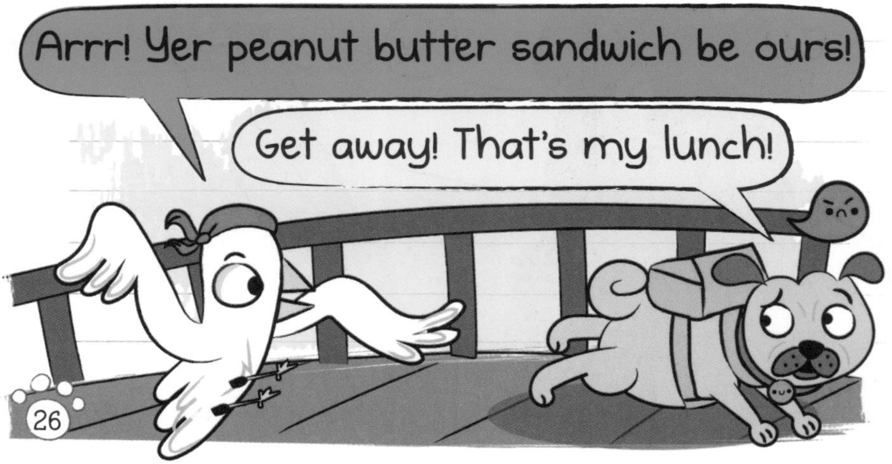
Arrr! Yer peanut butter sandwich be ours!
Get away! That's my lunch!

Luna climbed up the steps to save me.

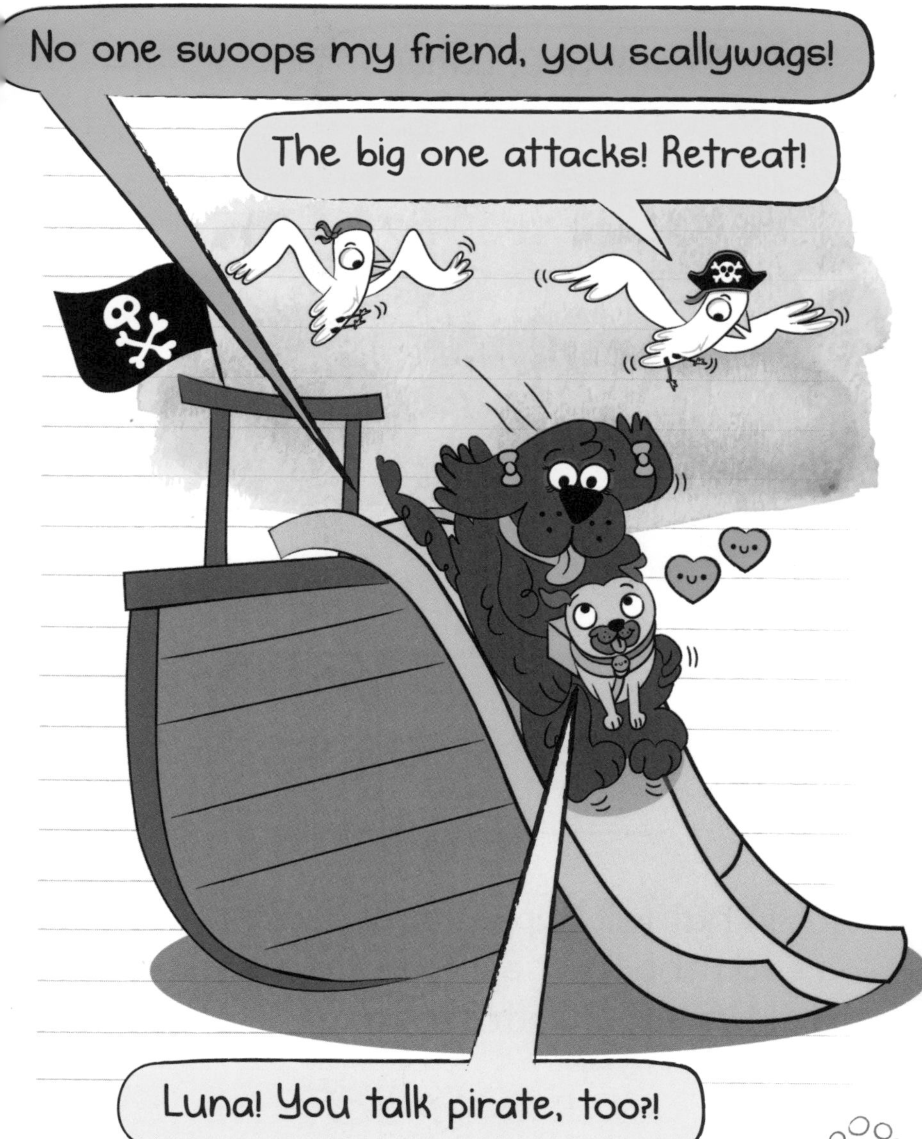
No one swoops my friend, you scallywags!
The big one attacks! Retreat!
Luna! You talk pirate, too?!

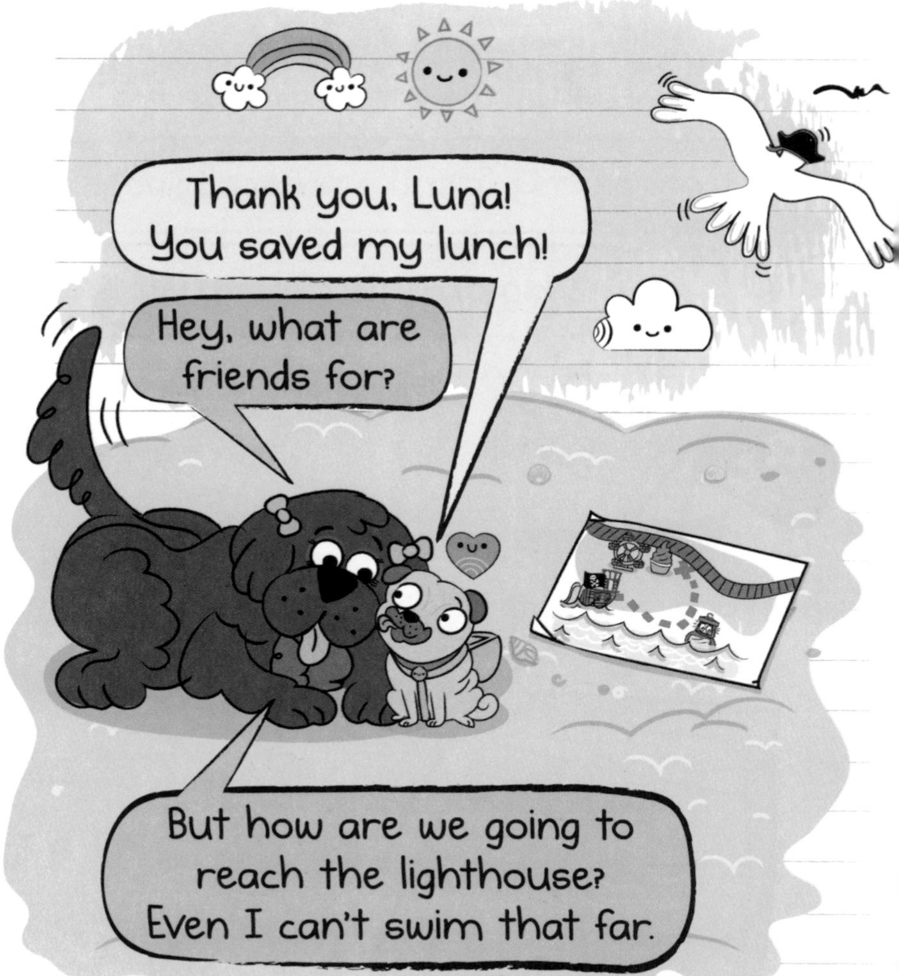
Thank you, Luna! You saved my lunch!
Hey, what are friends for?
But how are we going to reach the lighthouse? Even I can't swim that far.

What will happen now, Diary? If we can't reach the next spot on the map, does that mean our treasure hunt is over?

Chapter 4

LOW-TIDE BEACH SURPRISE

THURSDAY

Dear Diary,

This morning, Bella gave me an idea.

The tide's too low for surfing today, so we're going to search for seashells.

The tide?

That pirate seagull had said "tide" meant the "rise and fall" of the sea. Could that mean there would be less water today?

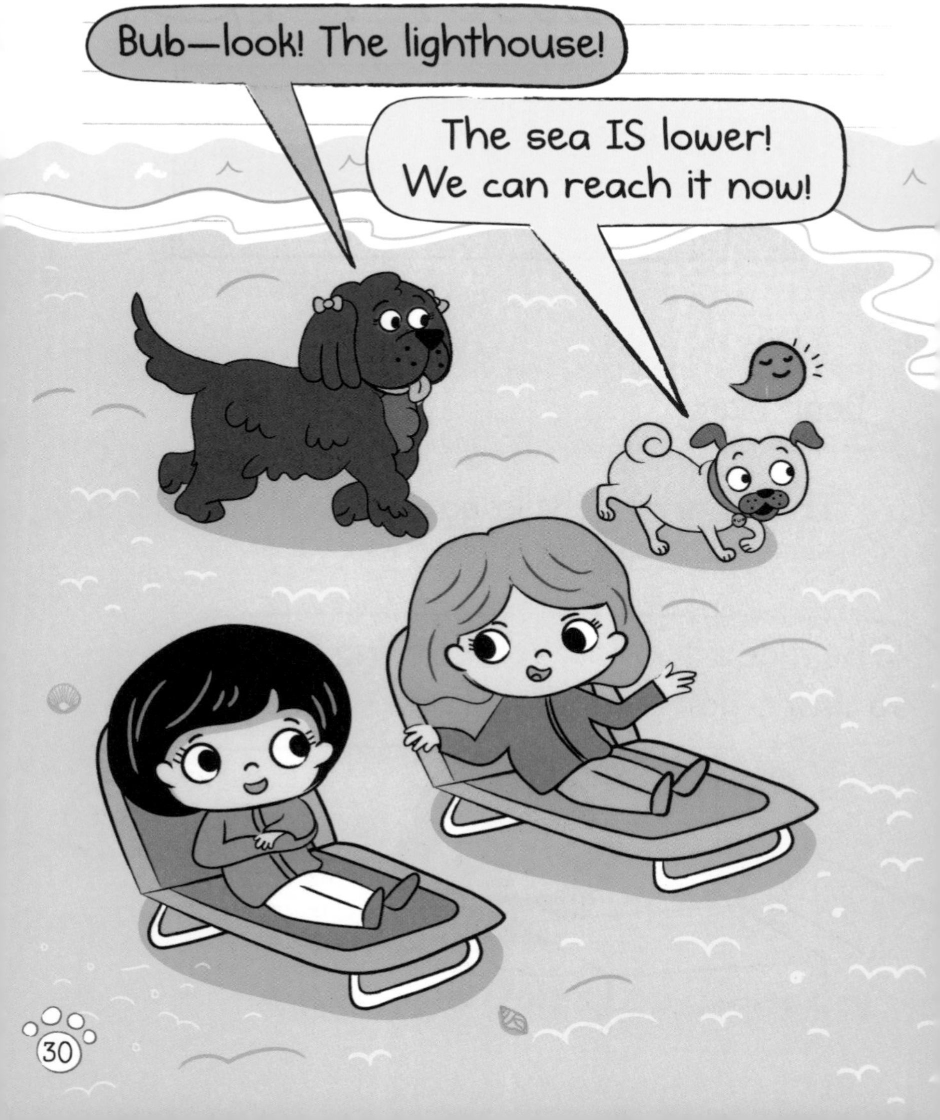
Bub—look! The lighthouse!
The sea IS lower!
We can reach it now!

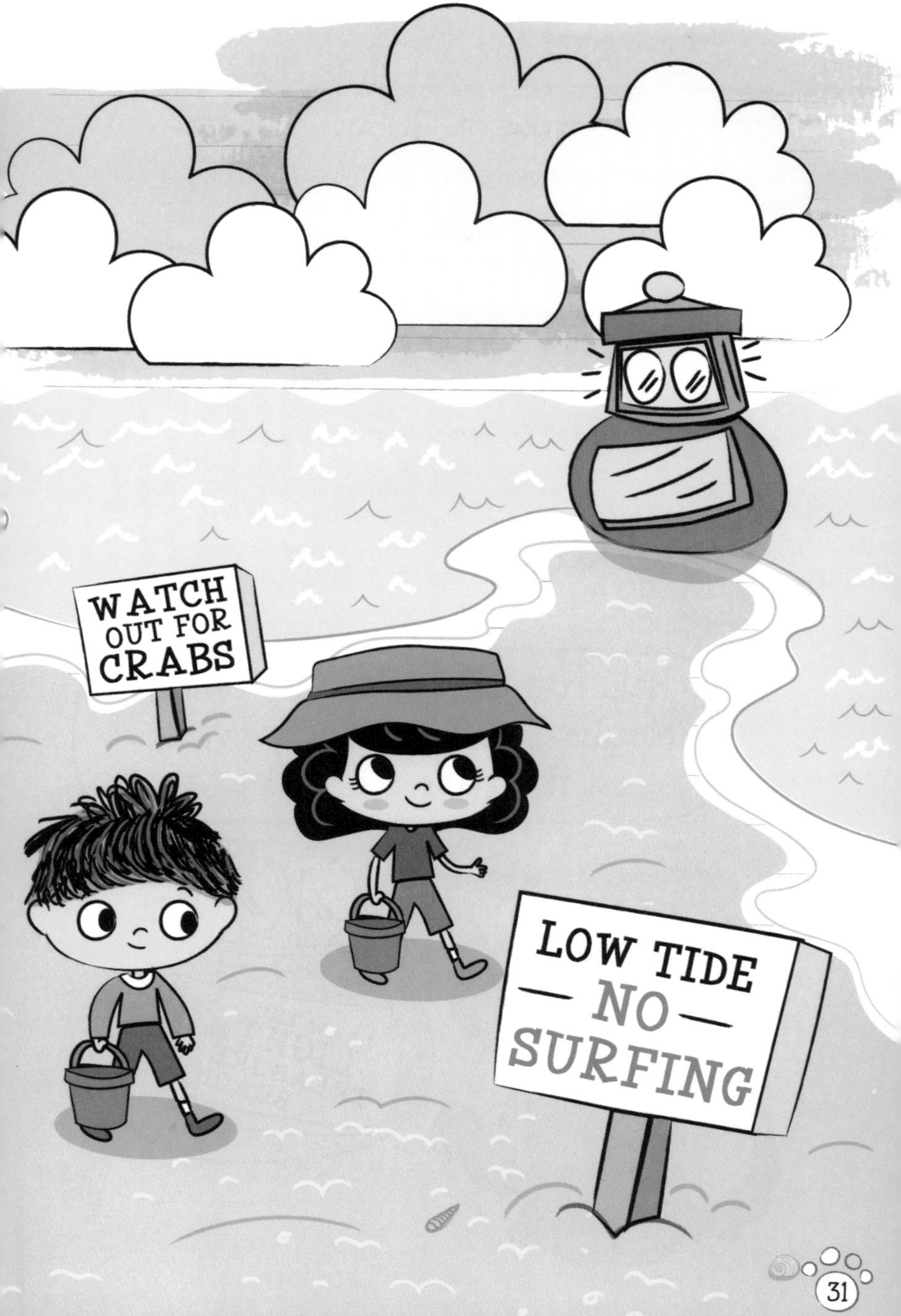
WATCH OUT FOR CRABS
LOW TIDE —NO— SURFING

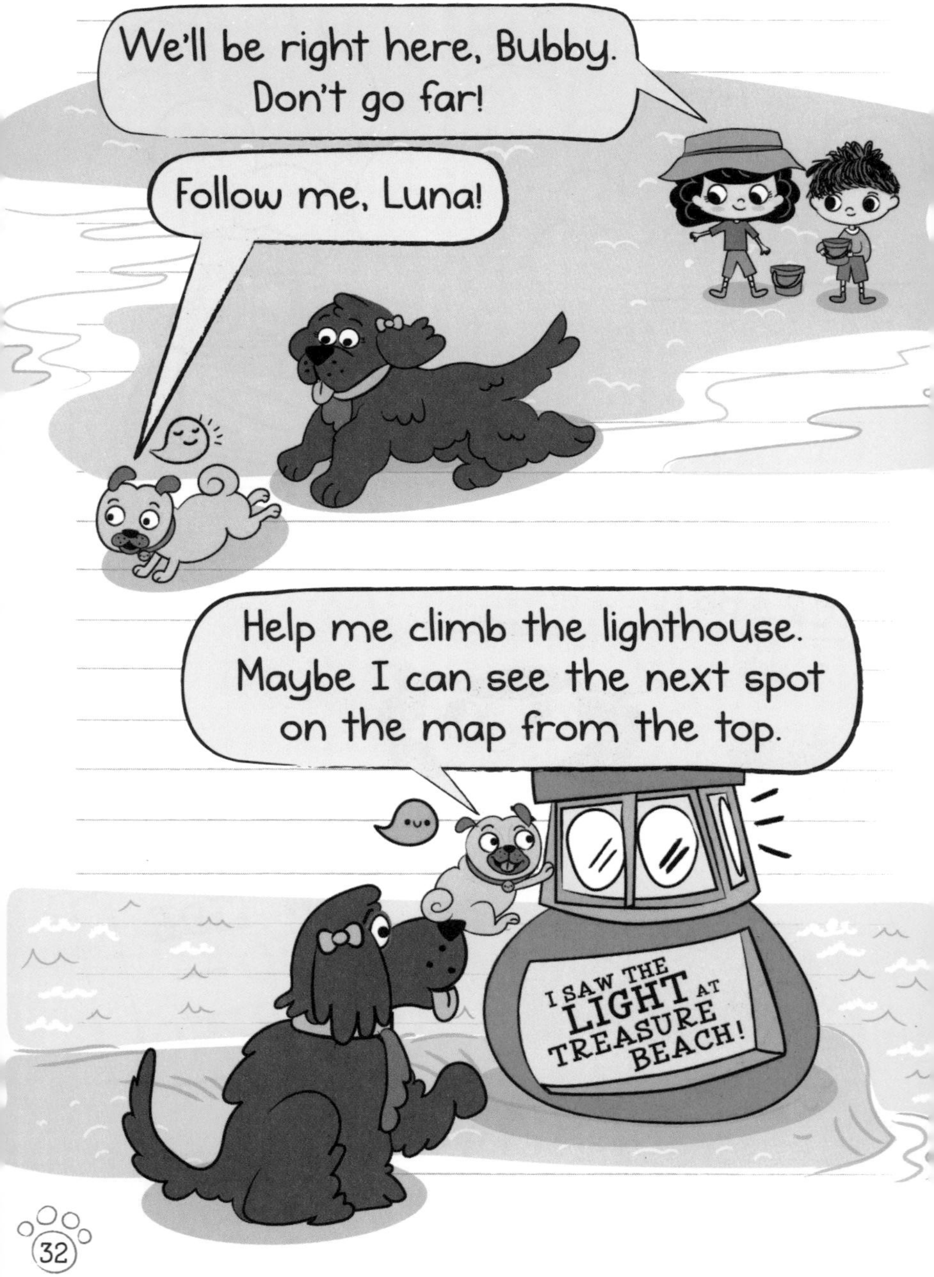
We'll be right here, Bubby. Don't go far!
Follow me, Luna!
Help me climb the lighthouse. Maybe I can see the next spot on the map from the top.
I SAW THE LIGHT AT TREASURE BEACH!

I couldn't believe it, Diary. From the top of the lighthouse, I was able to see a Ferris wheel!

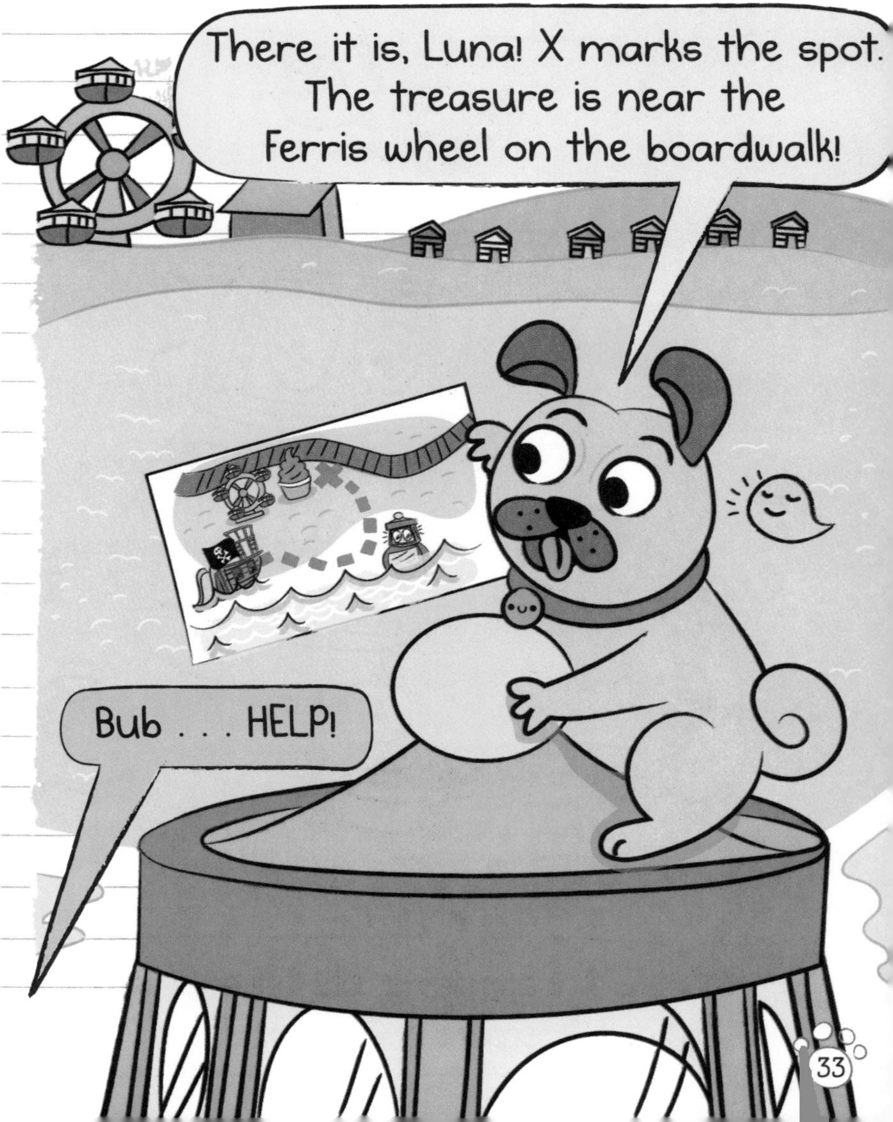
There it is, Luna! X marks the spot. The treasure is near the Ferris wheel on the boardwalk!
Bub . . . HELP!

Ack! Where did THOSE come from?
The low tide must bring CRABS!
W THE IGHT AT EASURE BEACH!
No trespassing! No trespassing! Prepare to be pinched!

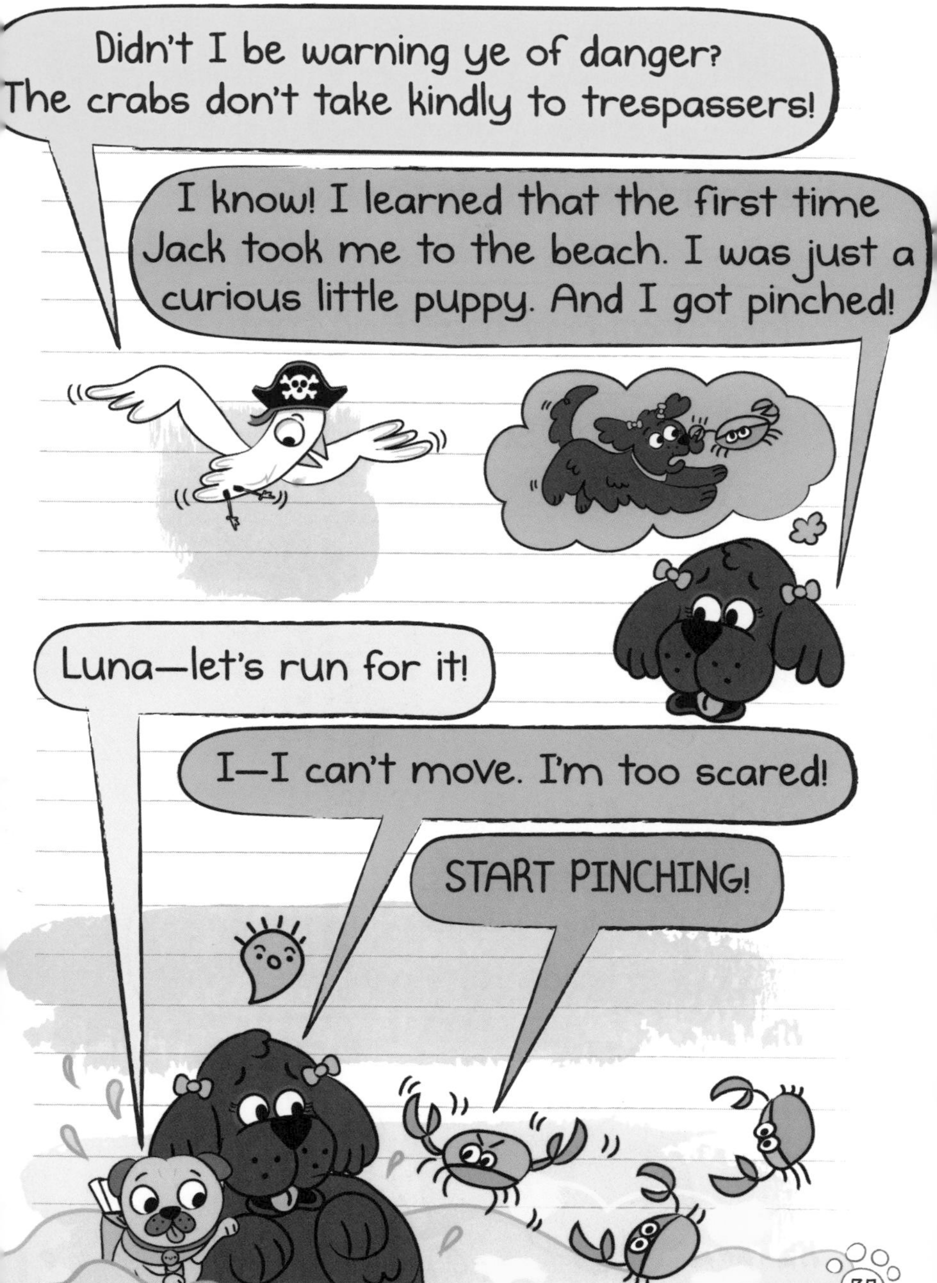

Didn't I be warning ye of danger? The crabs don't take kindly to trespassers!
I know! I learned that the first time Jack took me to the beach. I was just a curious little puppy. And I got pinched!
Luna—let's run for it!
I—I can't move. I'm too scared!
START PINCHING!

The crabs were scary, Diary. But I had to be brave. Luna needed my help! I did the only thing I could think of.

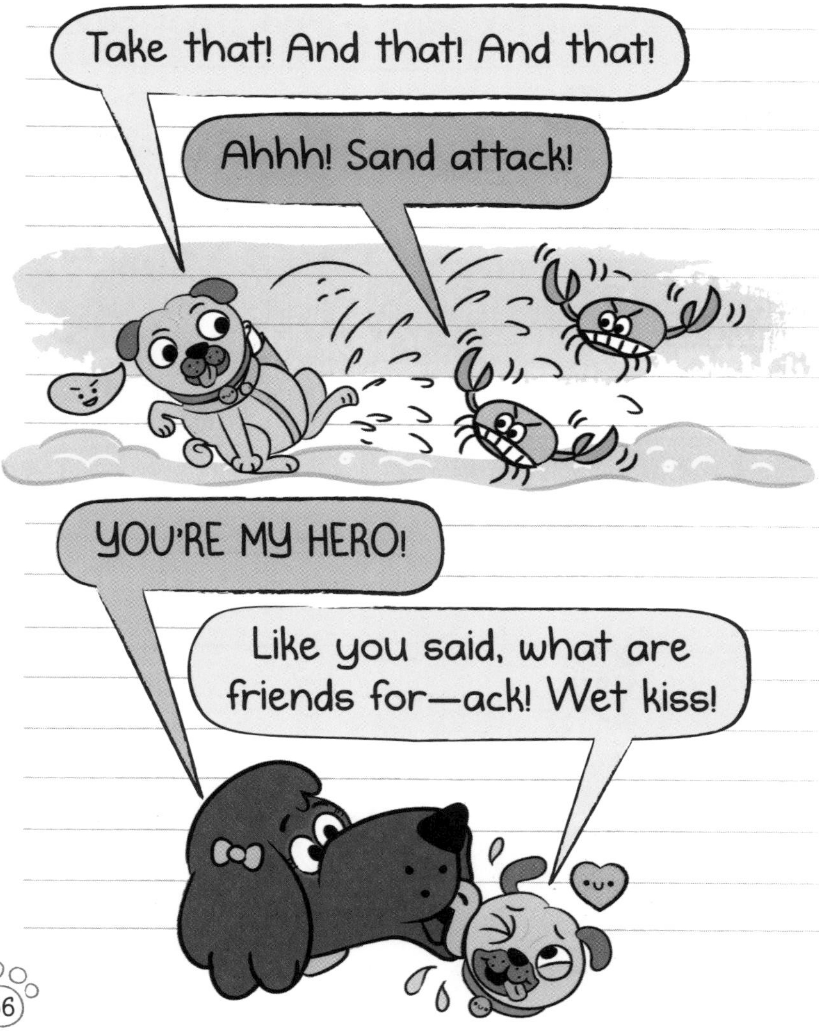
Take that! And that! And that!
Ahhh! Sand attack!
YOU'RE MY HERO!
Like you said, what are friends for—ack! Wet kiss!

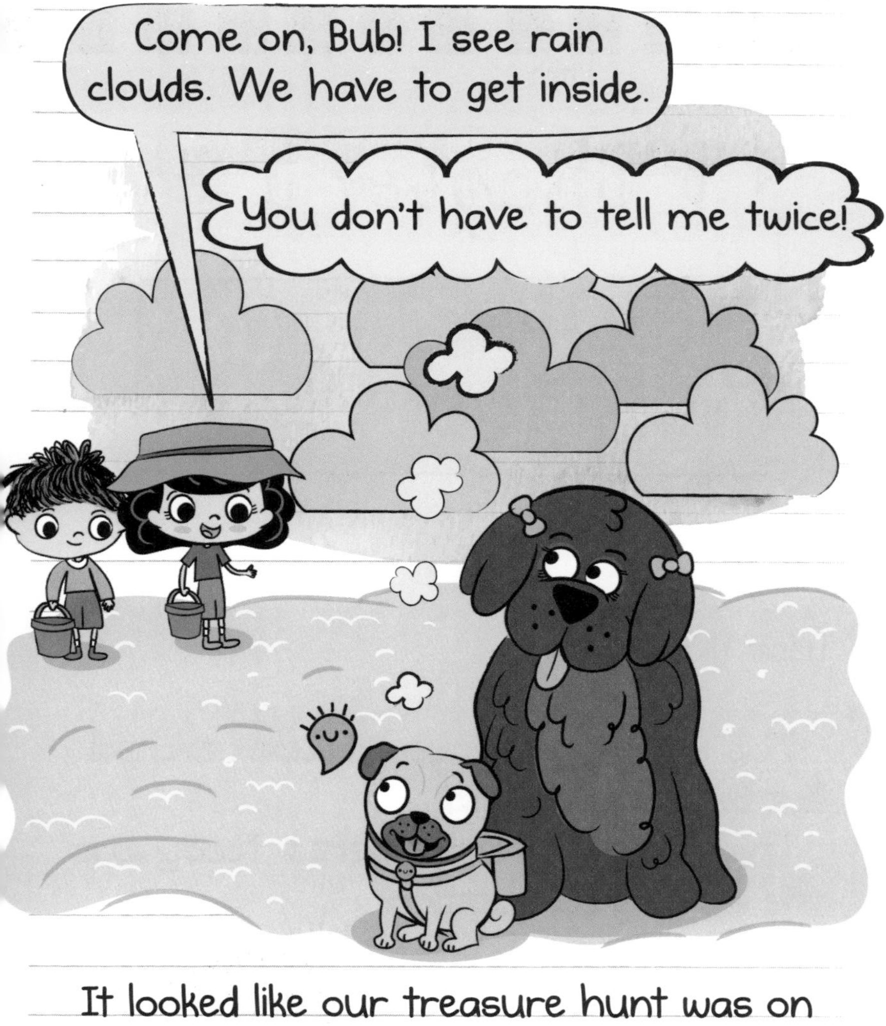
Come on, Bub! I see rain clouds. We have to get inside.
You don't have to tell me twice!

It looked like our treasure hunt was on hold again. But tomorrow, Diary, we'll visit the boardwalk and find that treasure for sure!

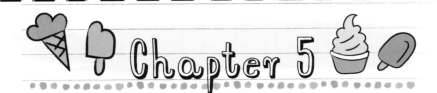

Chapter 5

BEACH YOU TO THE BOARDWALK

FRIDAY MORNING

Dear Diary,

This morning, I woke up super excited! But Bella seemed sad.

That's when I remembered: Today was the surfing competition.

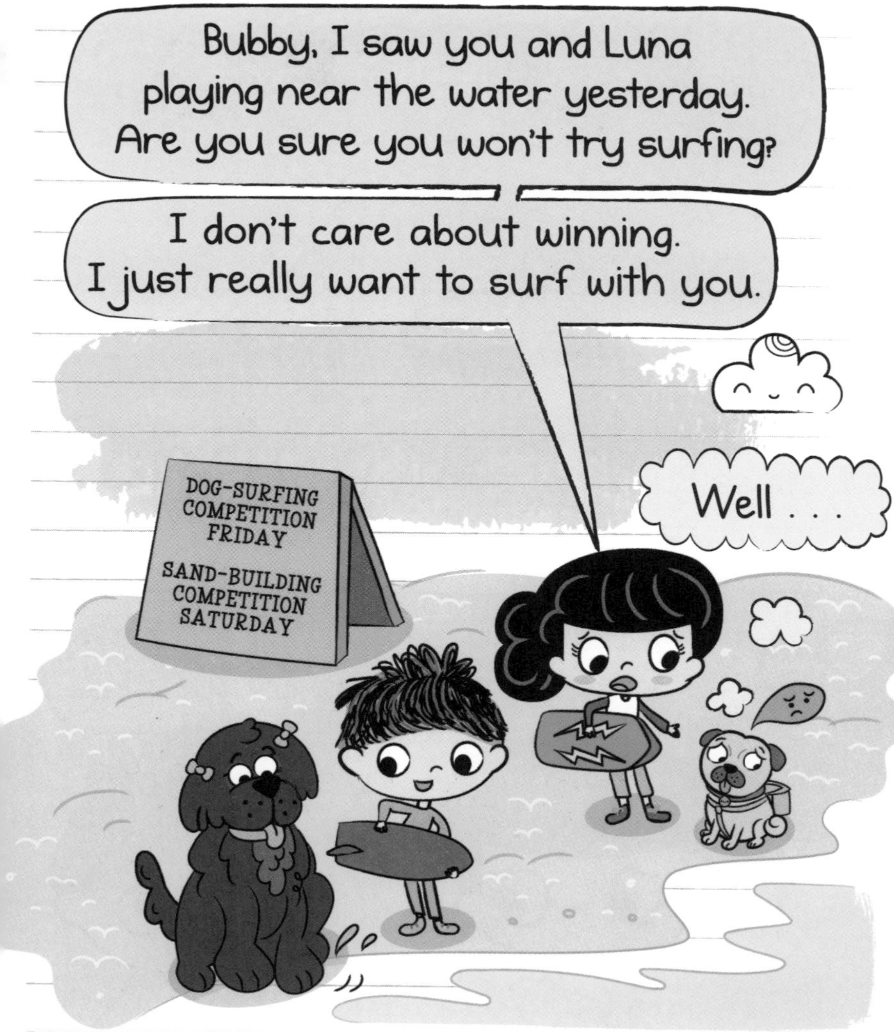
Bubby, I saw you and Luna playing near the water yesterday. Are you sure you won't try surfing?
I don't care about winning. I just really want to surf with you.
DOG-SURFING COMPETITION FRIDAY
SAND-BUILDING COMPETITION SATURDAY
Well . . .

I didn't want Bella to be sad. Was there any way I could surf <u>without</u> getting wet?

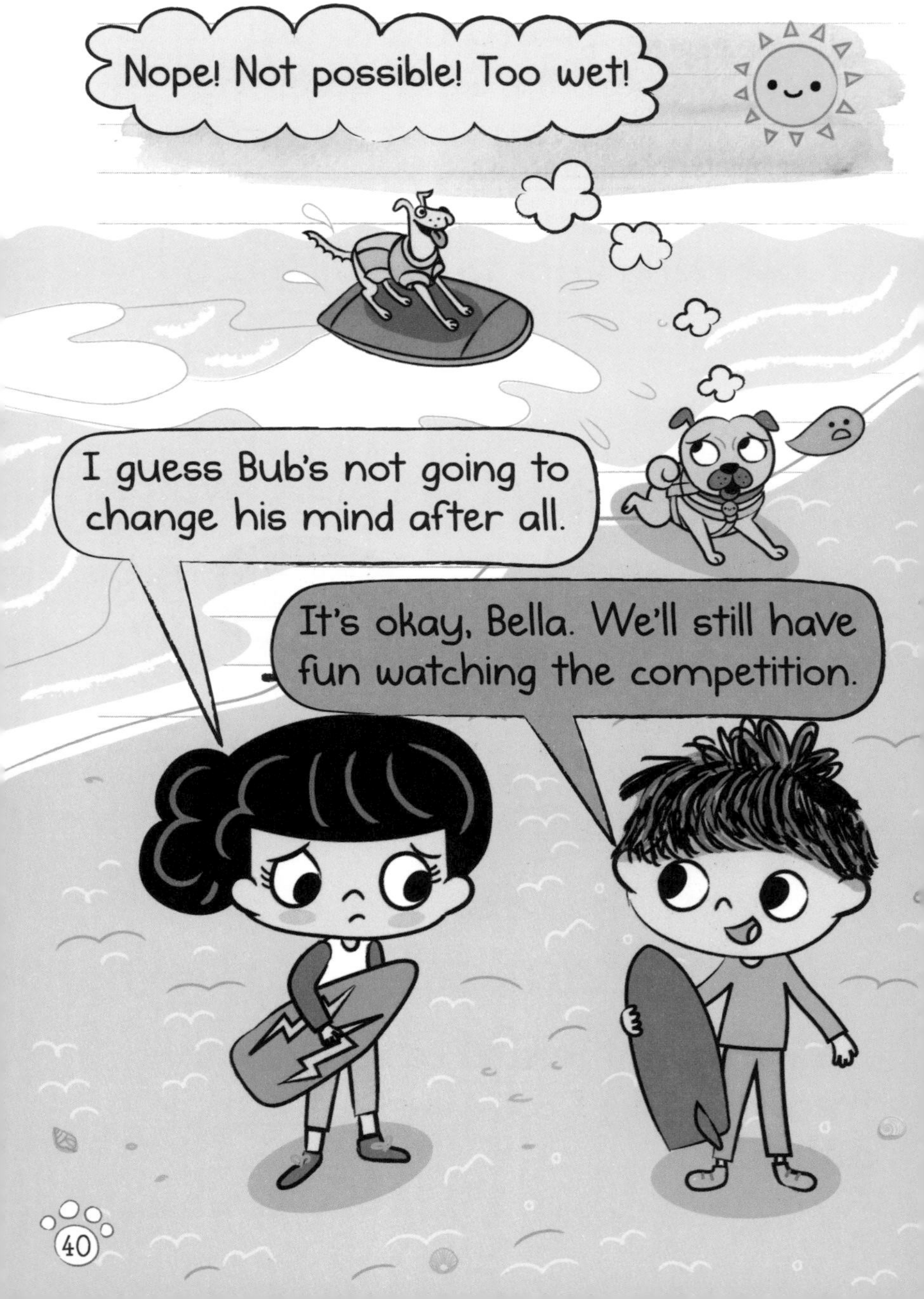
Nope! Not possible! Too wet!
I guess Bub's not going to change his mind after all.
It's okay, Bella. We'll still have fun watching the competition.

I felt terrible, Diary. I wished surfing didn't have so much water.

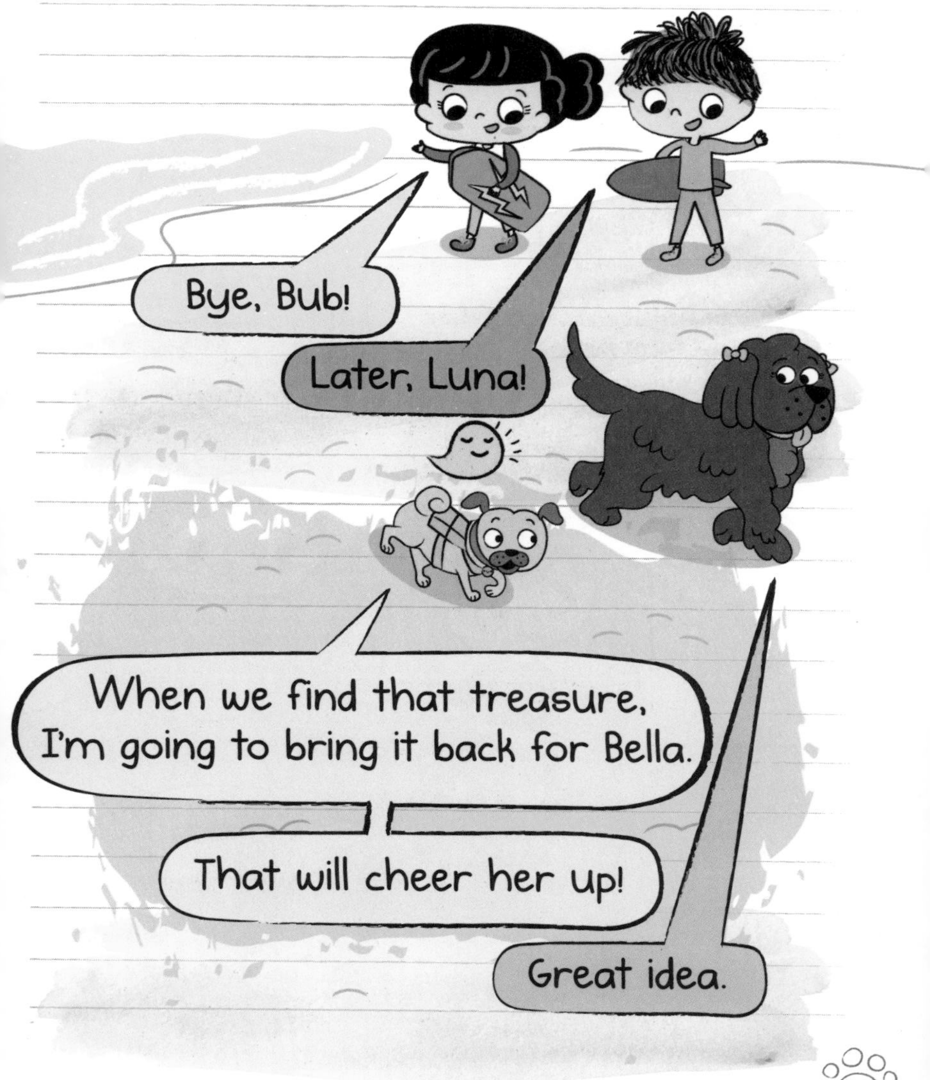
Bye, Bub!
Later, Luna!
When we find that treasure, I'm going to bring it back for Bella.
That will cheer her up!
Great idea.

Luna and I reached the boardwalk . . .

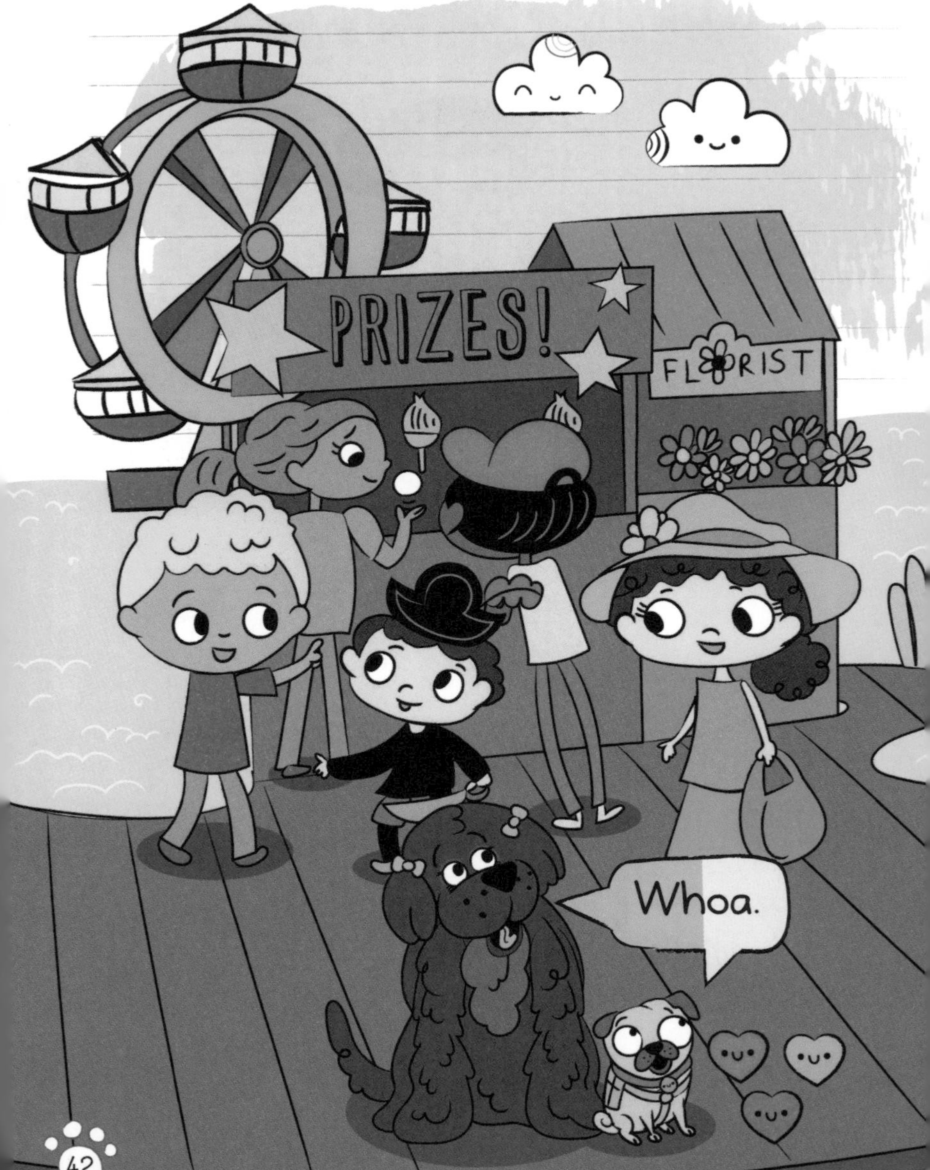
PRIZES!
FLORIST
Whoa.

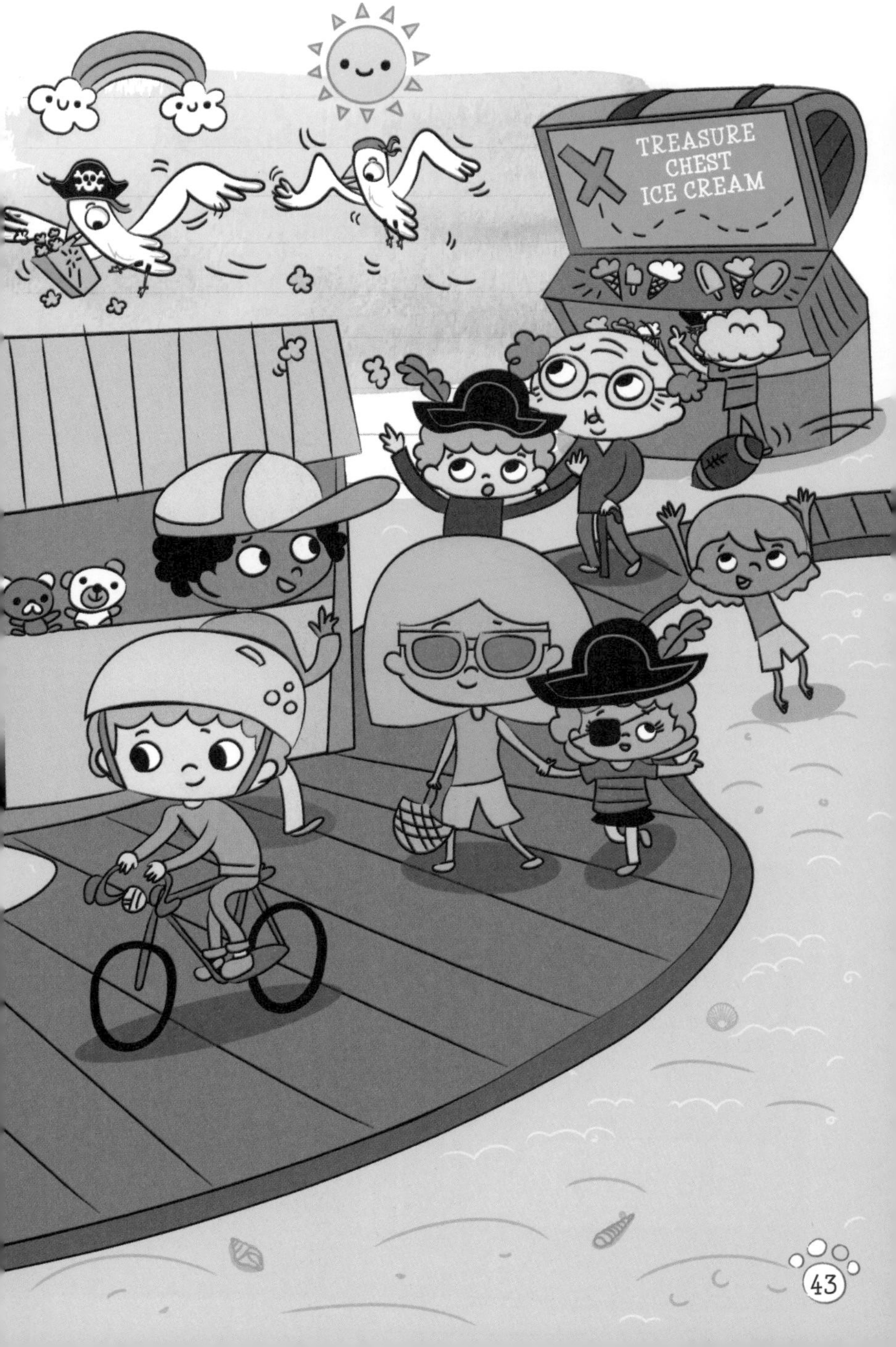
TREASURE
CHEST
ICE CREAM

But reaching X Marks the Spot was going to be trickier than we thought!

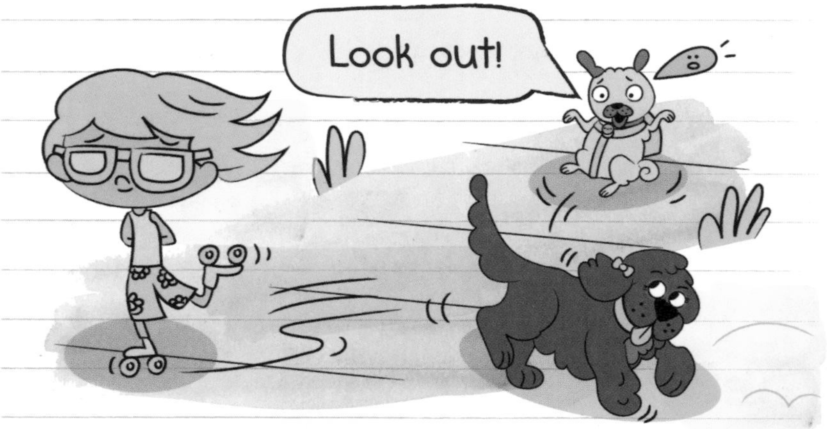
Look out!

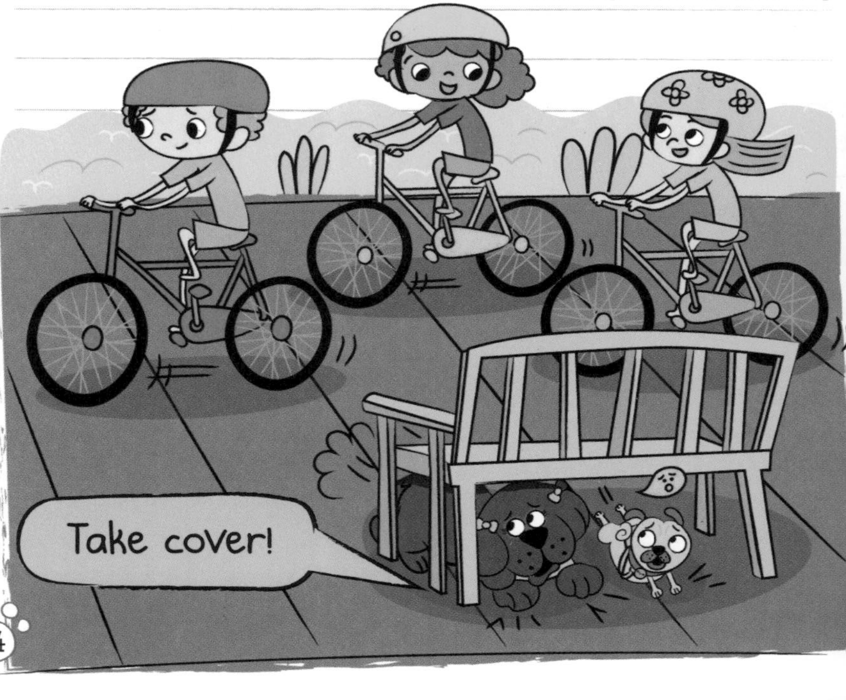
Take cover!

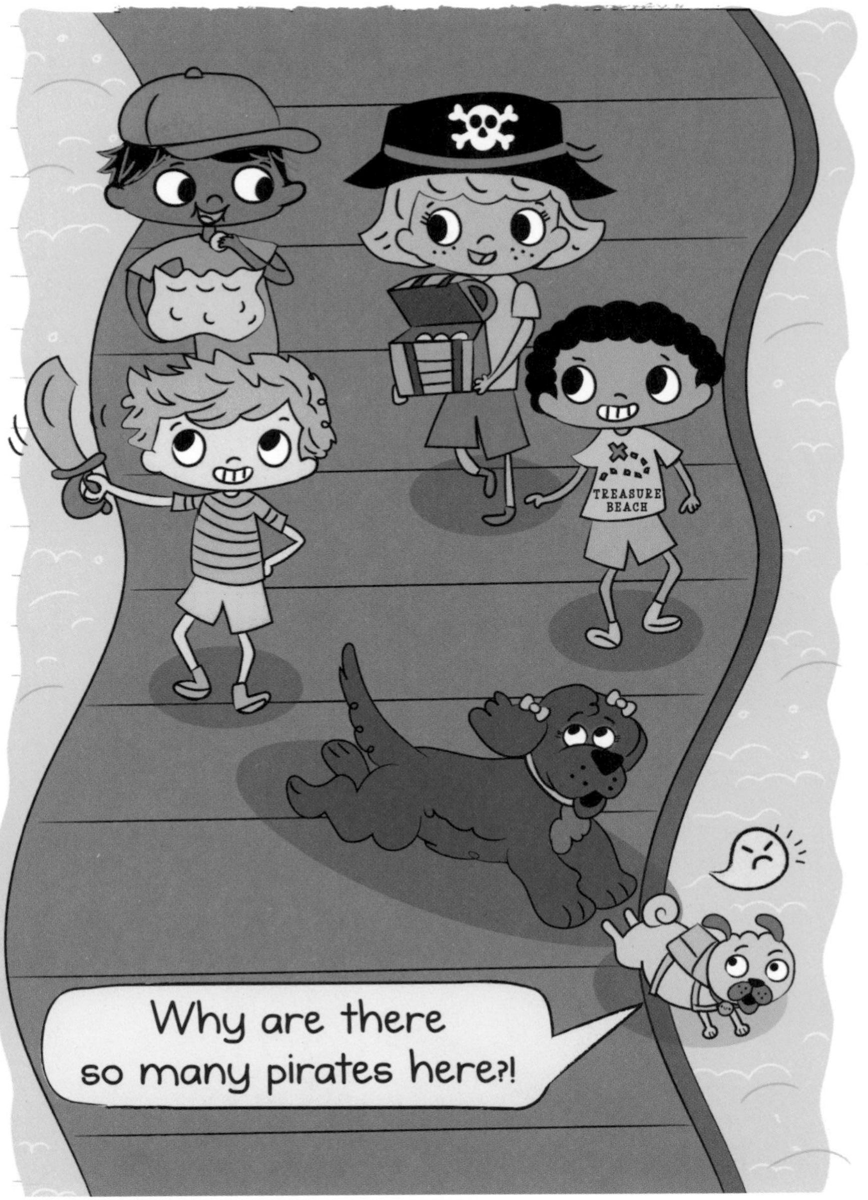
TREASURE
BEACH
Why are there
so many pirates here?!

Finally, Diary, we reached the X. And we found the treasure chest!

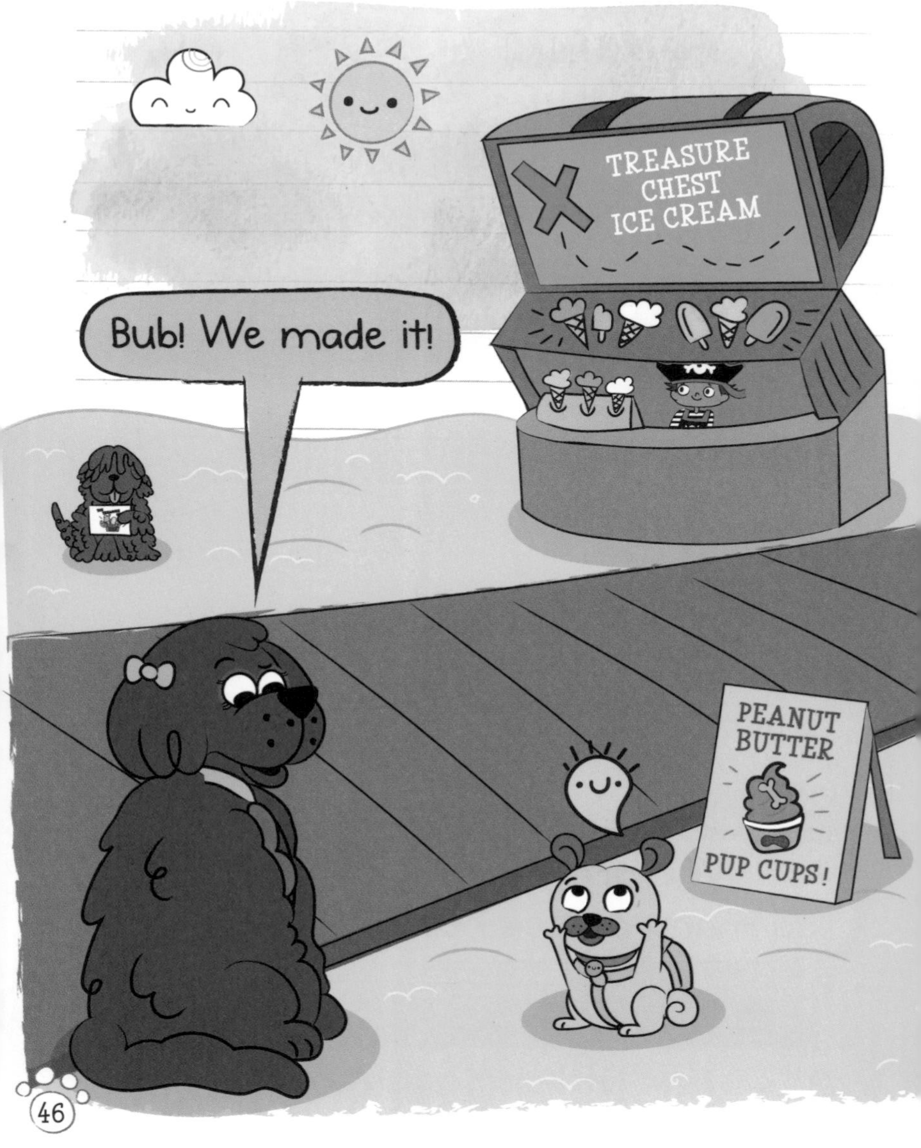
TREASURE
CHEST
ICE CREAM
Bub! We made it!
PEANUT
BUTTER
PUP CUPS!

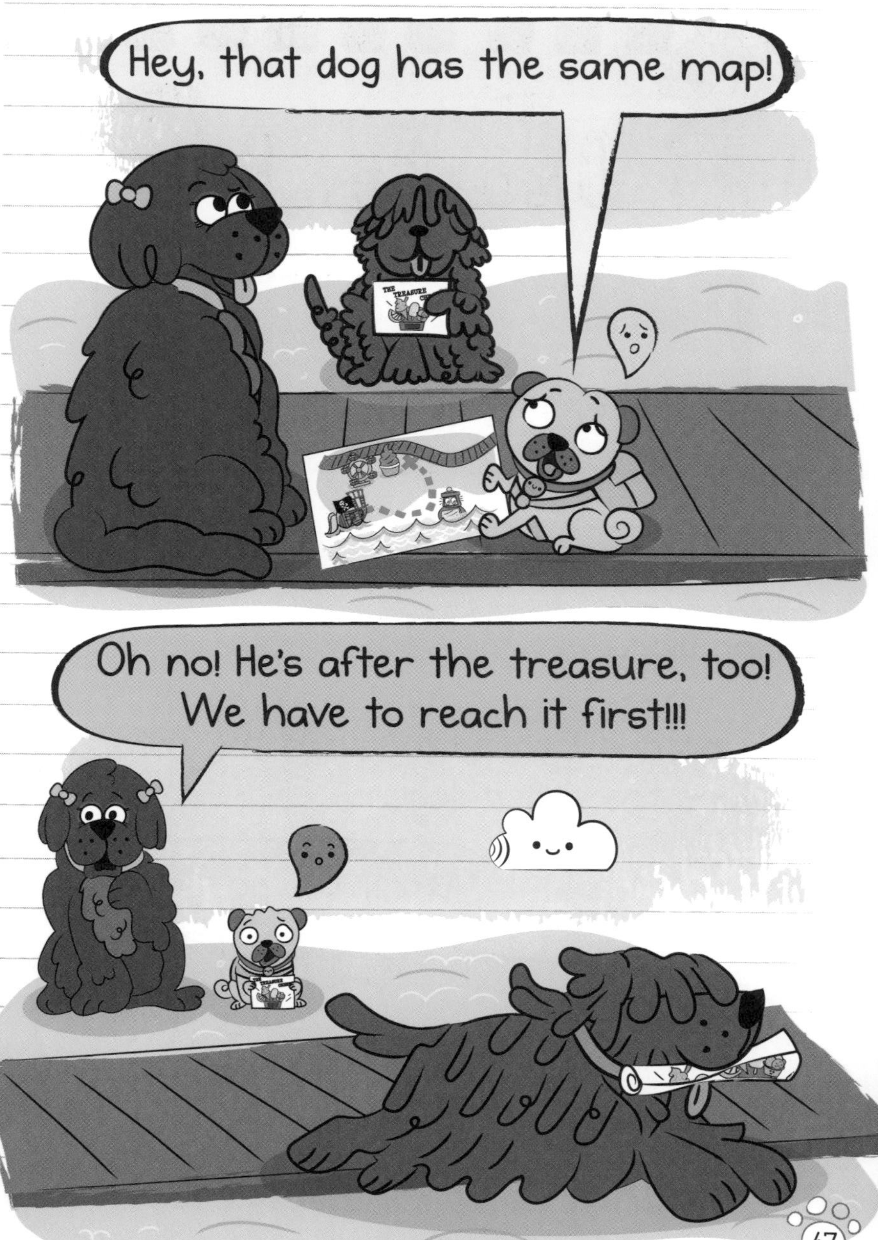
Hey, that dog has the same map!
Oh no! He's after the treasure, too! We have to reach it first!!!

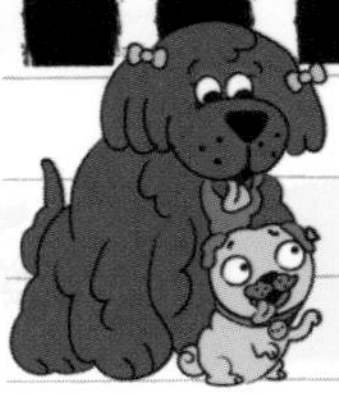

Chapter 6

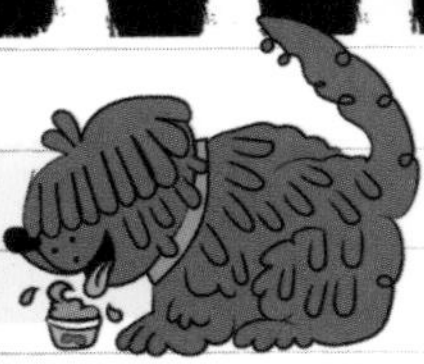

THE BEST BEACH TREASURE

FRIDAY MIDDAY

Dear Diary,

Luna and I raced to reach the treasure before the other dog!

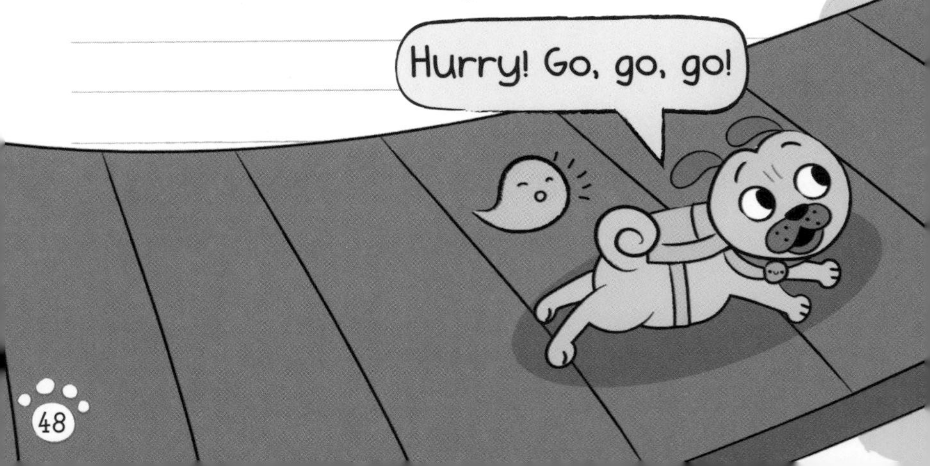
Hurry! Go, go, go!

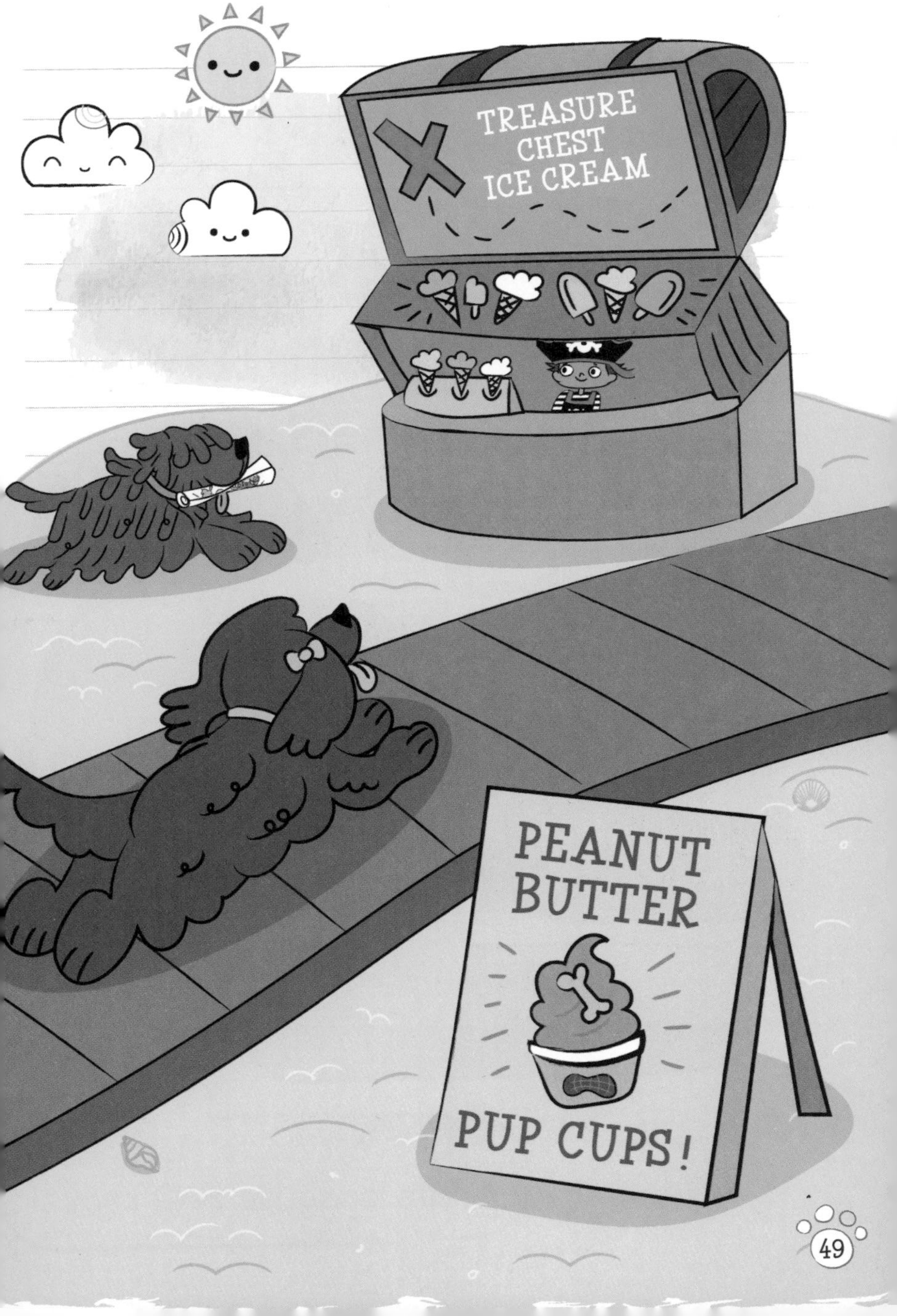
TREASURE CHEST ICE CREAM
PEANUT BUTTER
PUP CUPS!

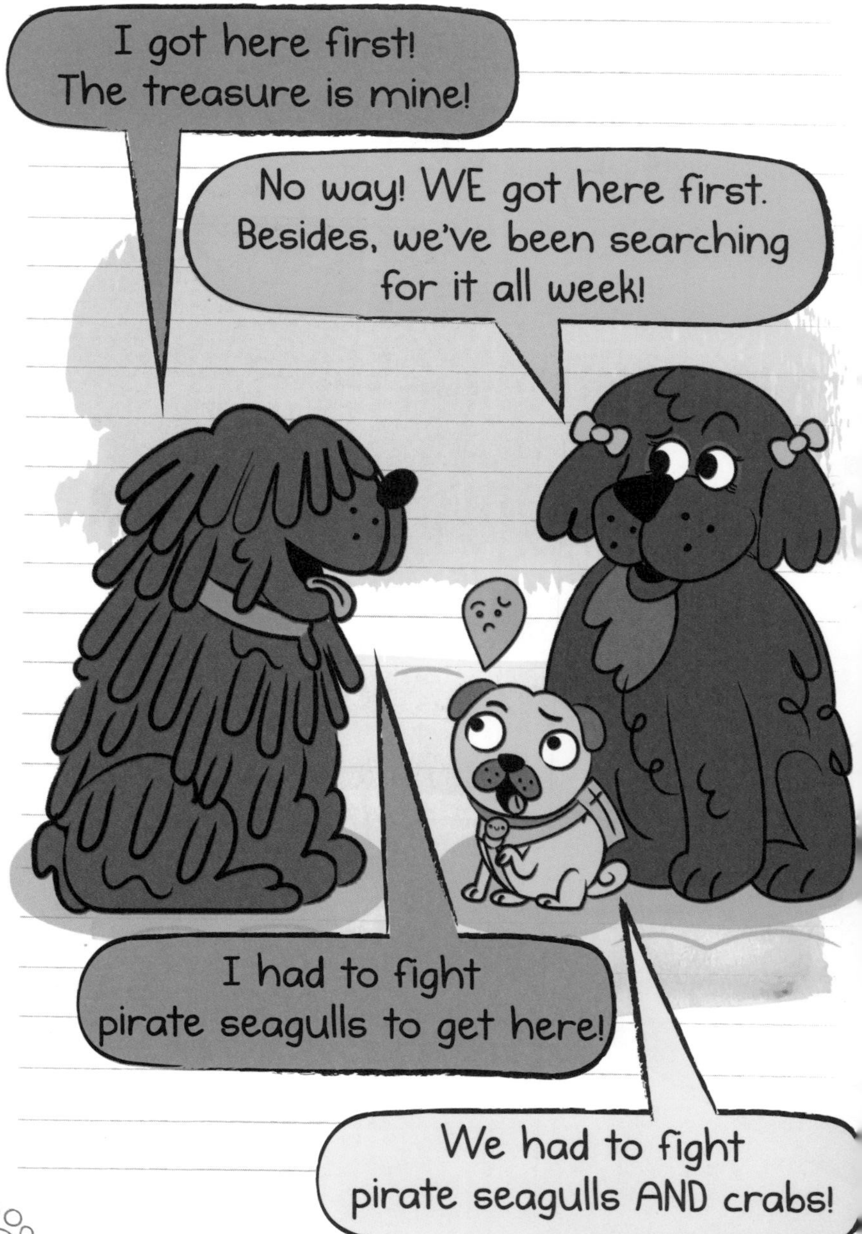
I got here first! The treasure is mine!
No way! WE got here first. Besides, we've been searching for it all week!
I had to fight pirate seagulls to get here!
We had to fight pirate seagulls AND crabs!

But as it turned out, the man guarding the ice-cream treasure said there was enough to go around!

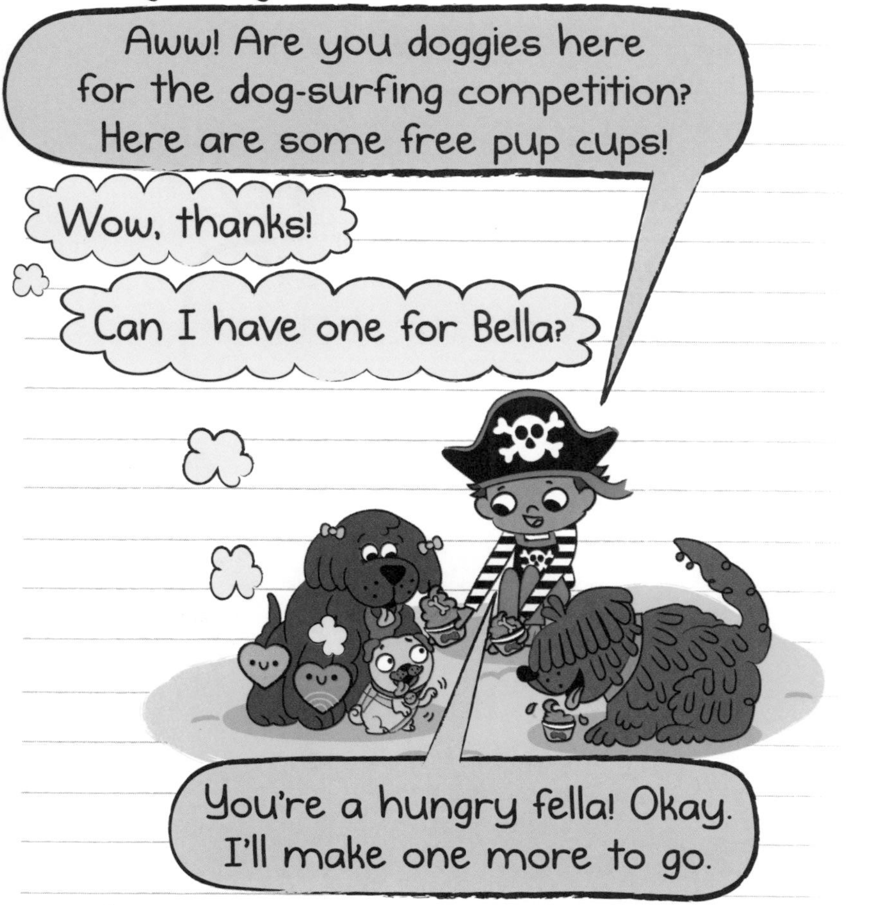
Aww! Are you doggies here for the dog-surfing competition? Here are some free pup cups!
Wow, thanks!
Can I have one for Bella?
You're a hungry fella! Okay. I'll make one more to go.

I had done it, Diary! I'd gotten the treasure for Bella! She would be so happy!

But just then, the other dog's owner showed up. And he said something that made me rethink everything.

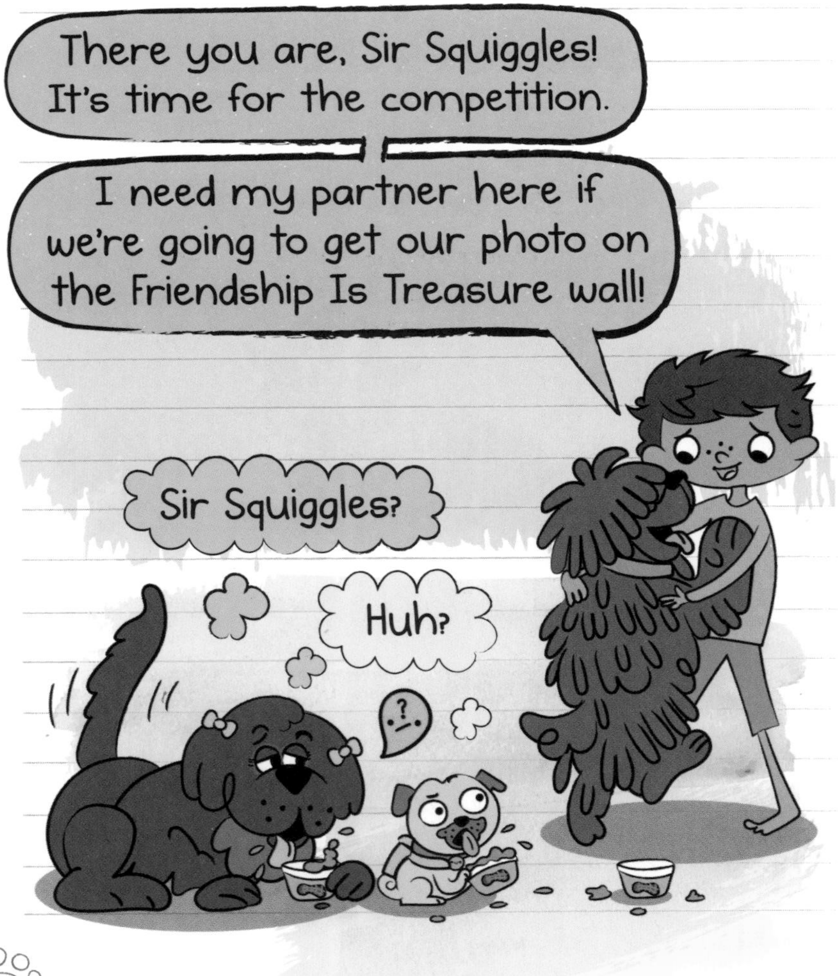
There you are, Sir Squiggles! It's time for the competition.
I need my partner here if we're going to get our photo on the Friendship Is Treasure wall!
Sir Squiggles?
Huh?
?

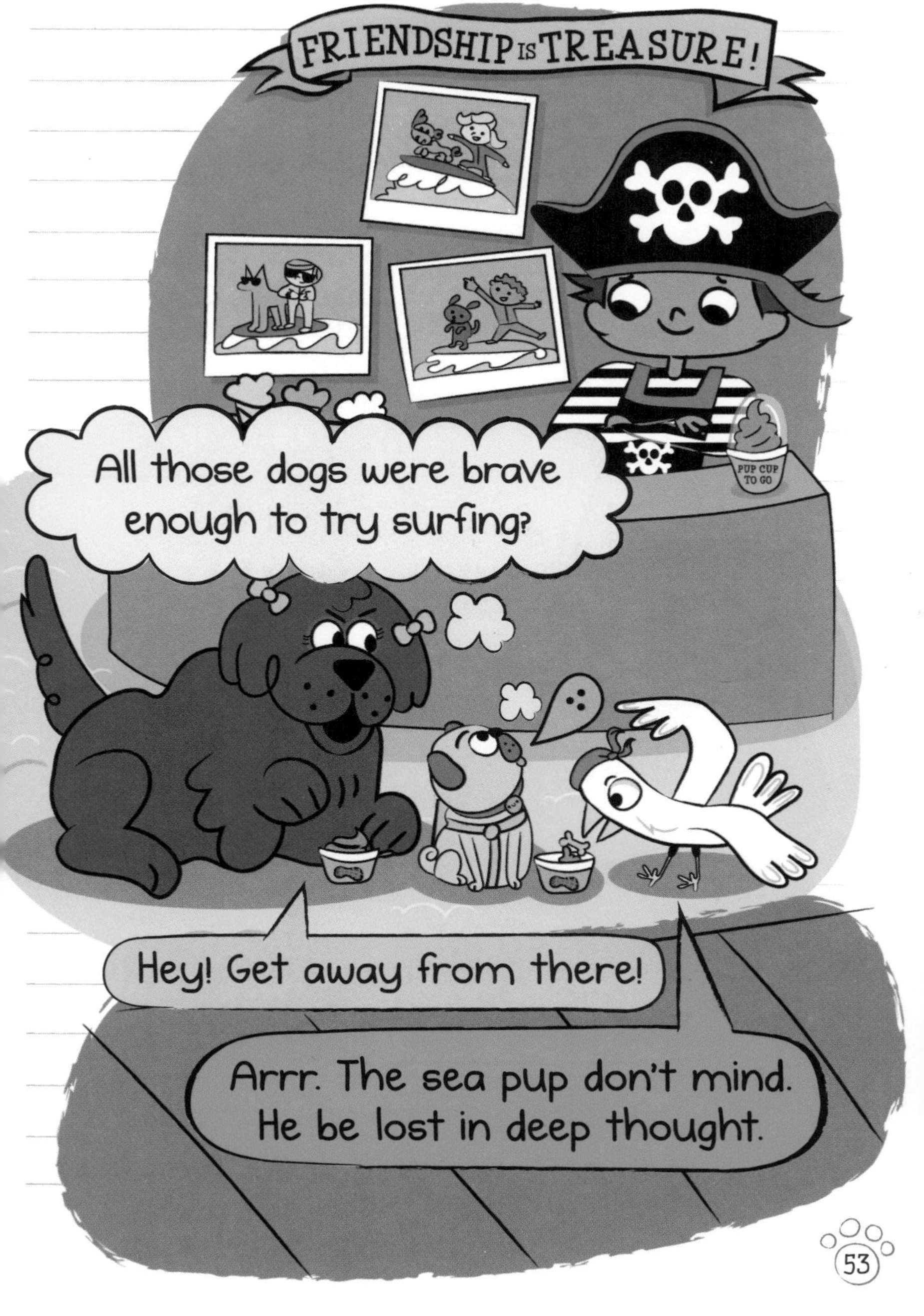
FRIENDSHIP IS TREASURE!
PUP CUP TO GO
All those dogs were brave enough to try surfing?
Hey! Get away from there!
Arrr. The sea pup don't mind. He be lost in deep thought.

Seeing those photos made me realize something, Diary.

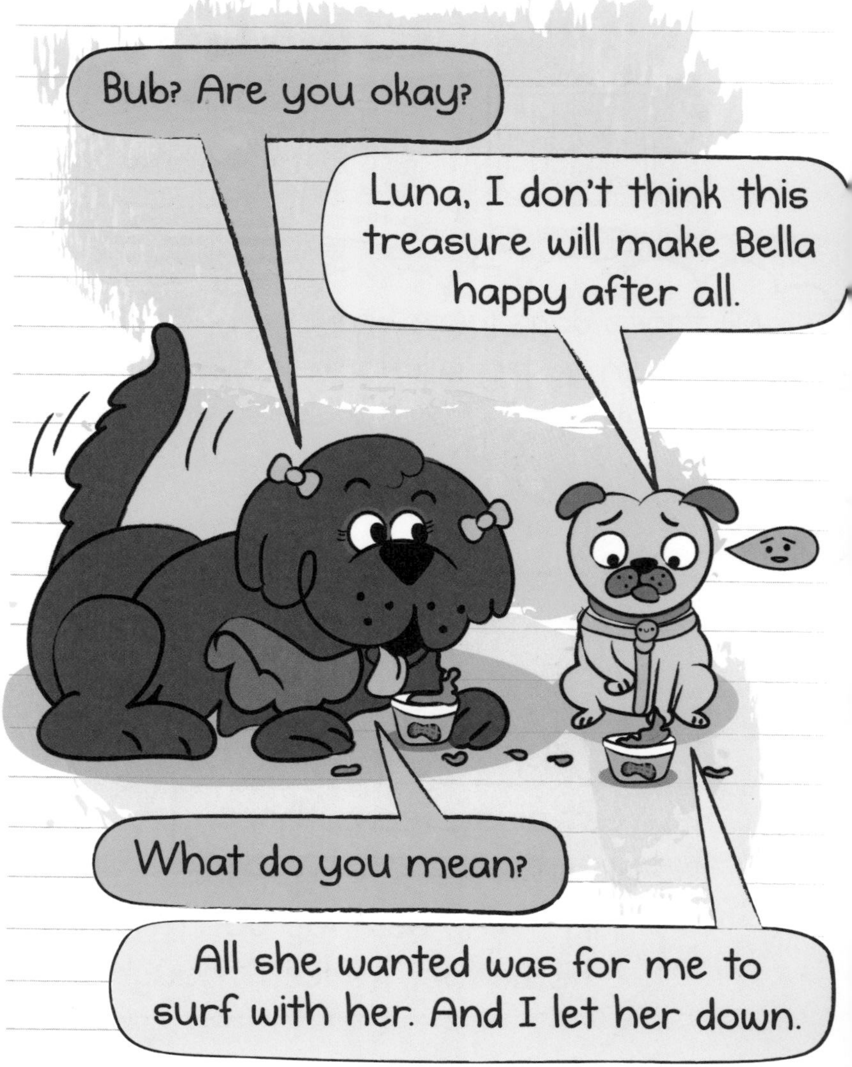
Bub? Are you okay?
Luna, I don't think this treasure will make Bella happy after all.
What do you mean?
All she wanted was for me to surf with her. And I let her down.

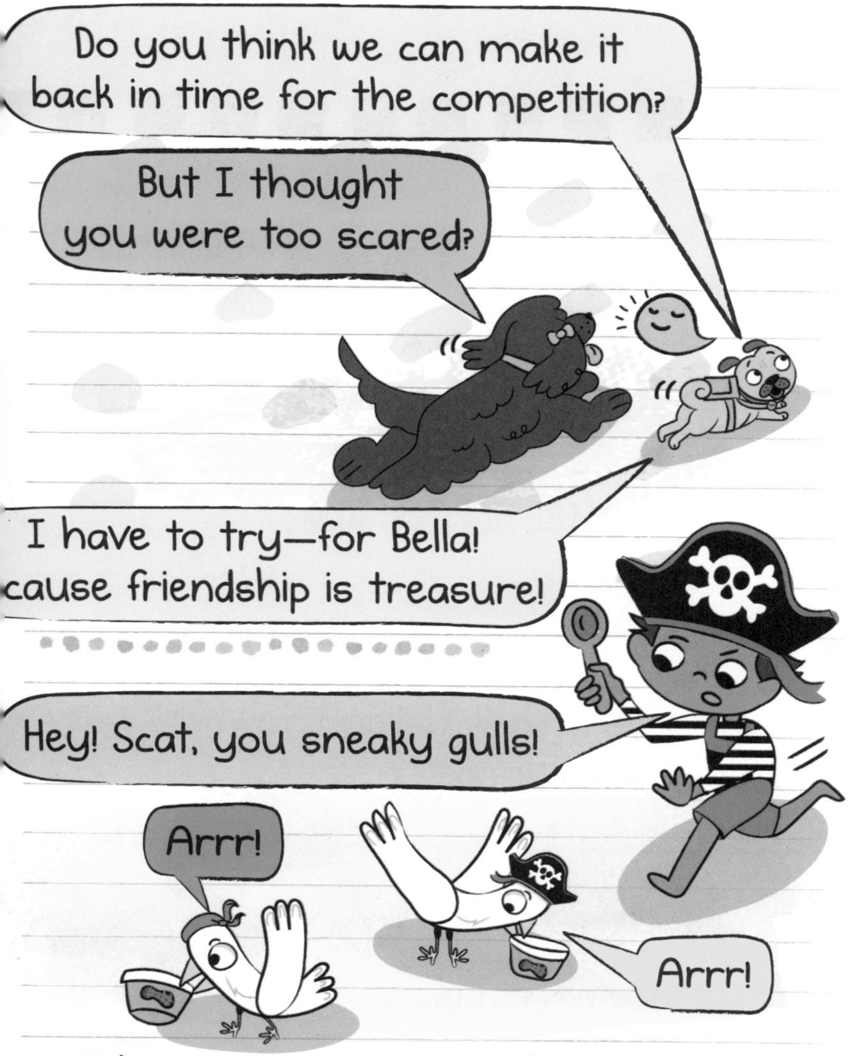
Do you think we can make it back in time for the competition?
But I thought you were too scared?
I have to try—for Bella! 'cause friendship is treasure!
Hey! Scat, you sneaky gulls!
Arrr!
Arrr!

If Luna was brave enough to fight pirates, and I was brave enough to battle crabs, . . . then maybe I was brave enough to surf after all?!

Chapter 7

A BRAVE BEACH IDEA

FRIDAY, COMPETITION TIME!

Dear Diary,

We made it back just in time! Bella was SO happy to see me!

Bub! There you are!

Wait . . . are you going to try surfing with me?

Let's do this!

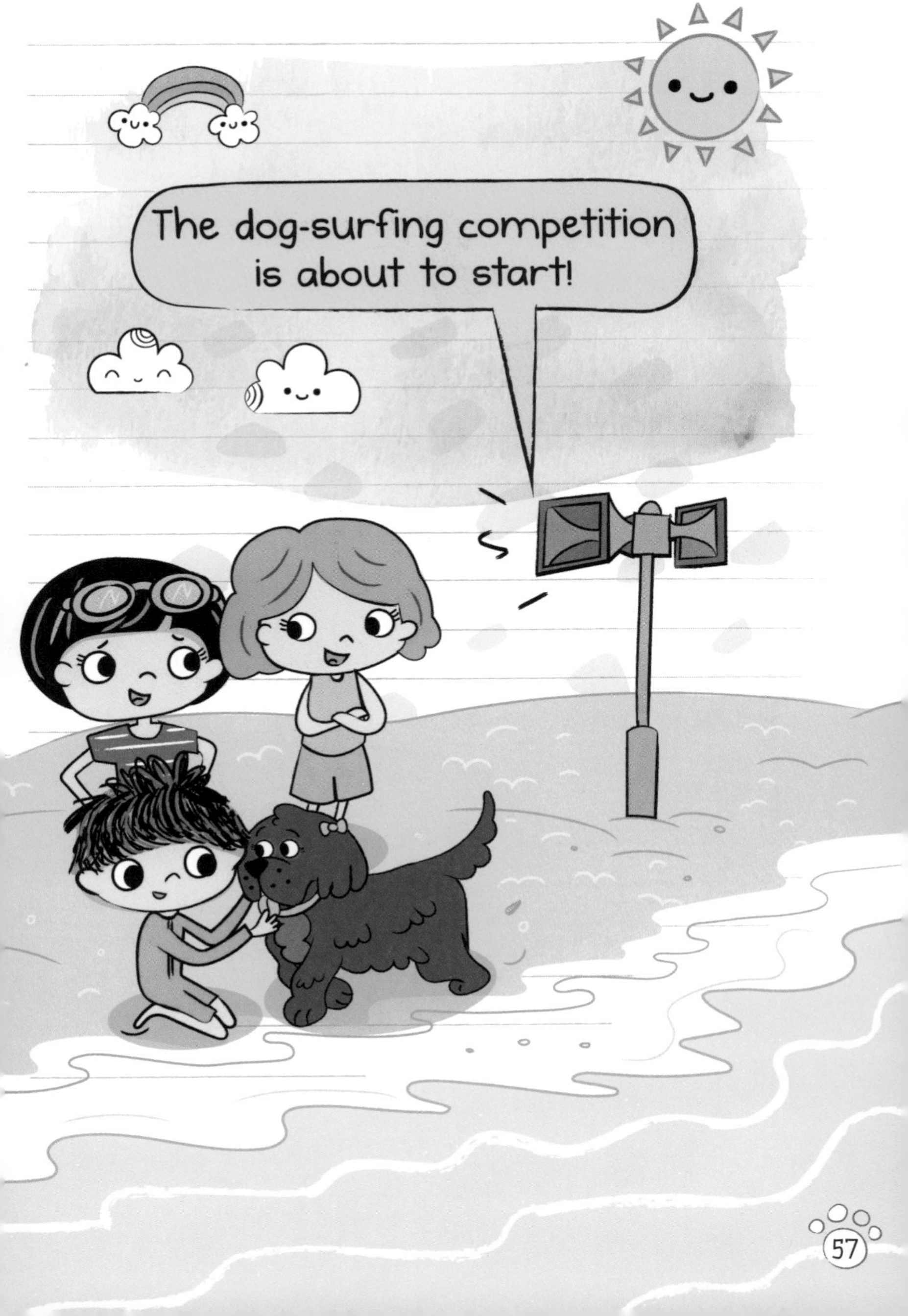
The dog-surfing competition is about to start!

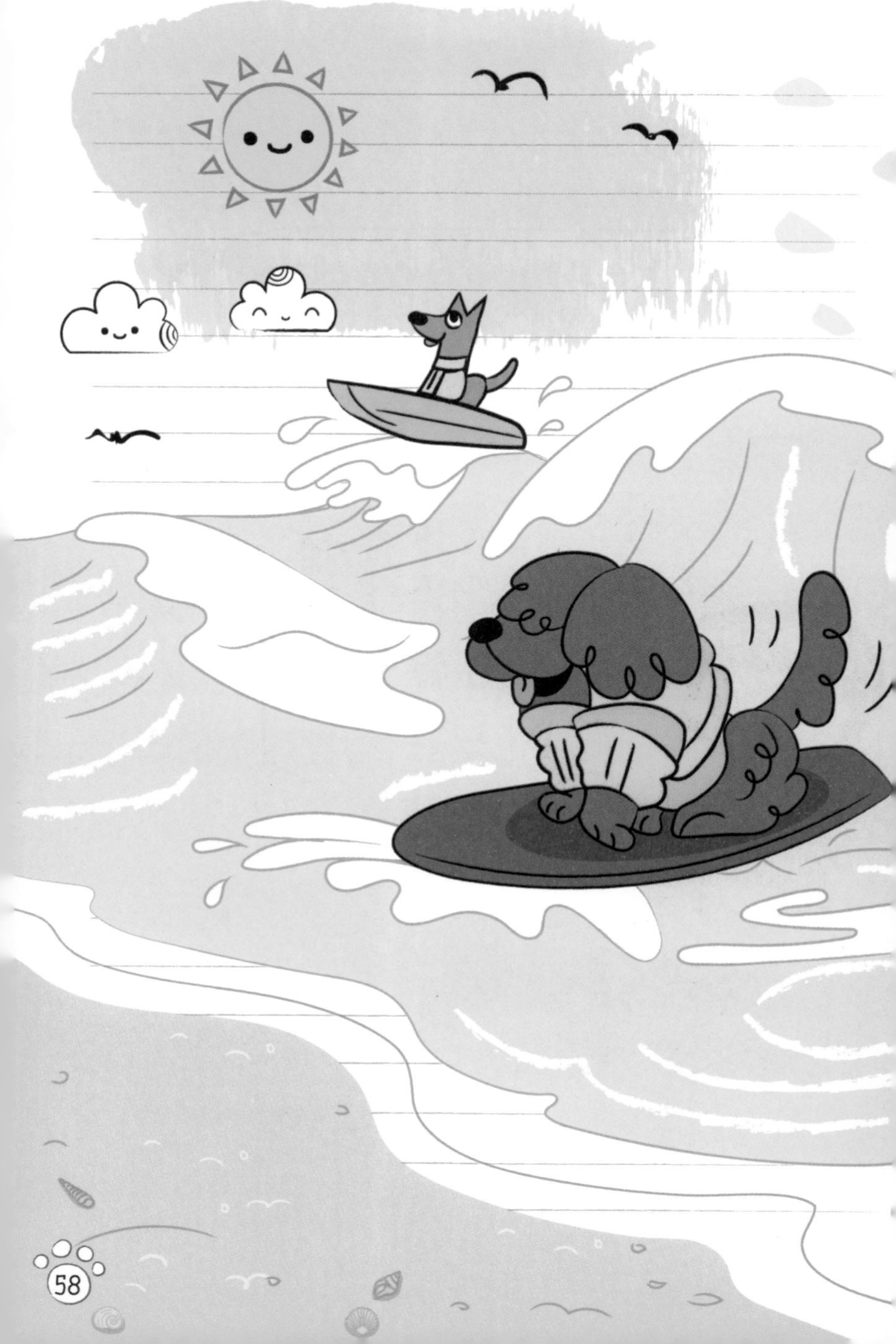

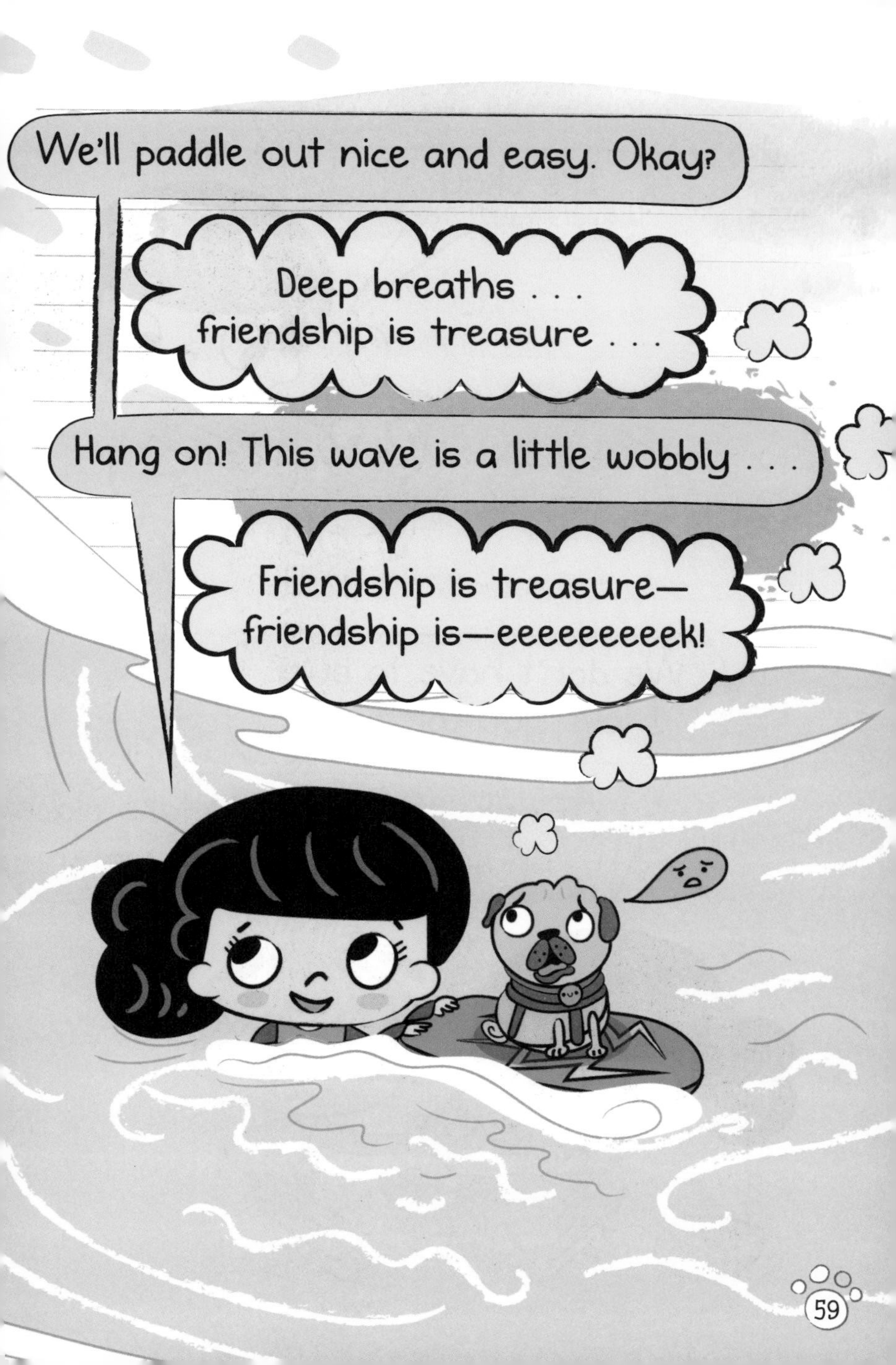

We'll paddle out nice and easy. Okay?
Deep breaths . . . friendship is treasure . . .
Hang on! This wave is a little wobbly . . .
Friendship is treasure— friendship is—eeeeeeeeek!

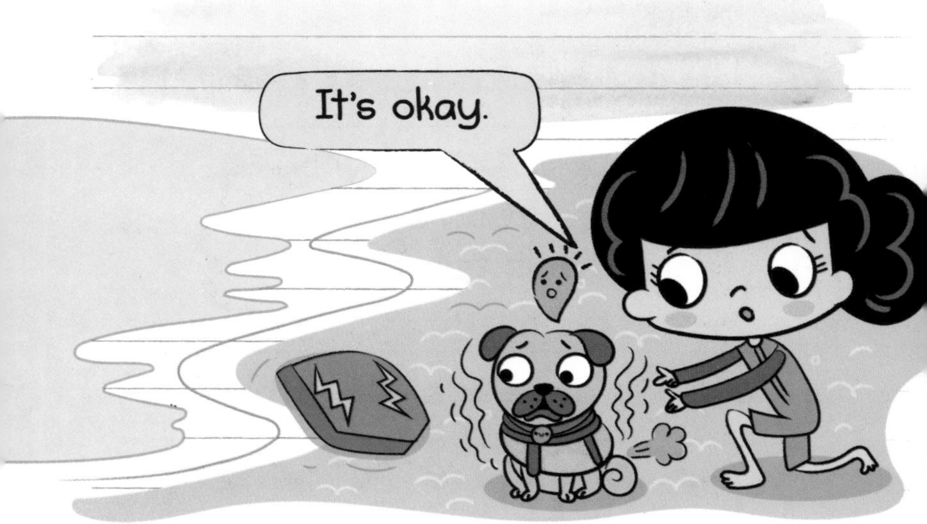
It's okay.

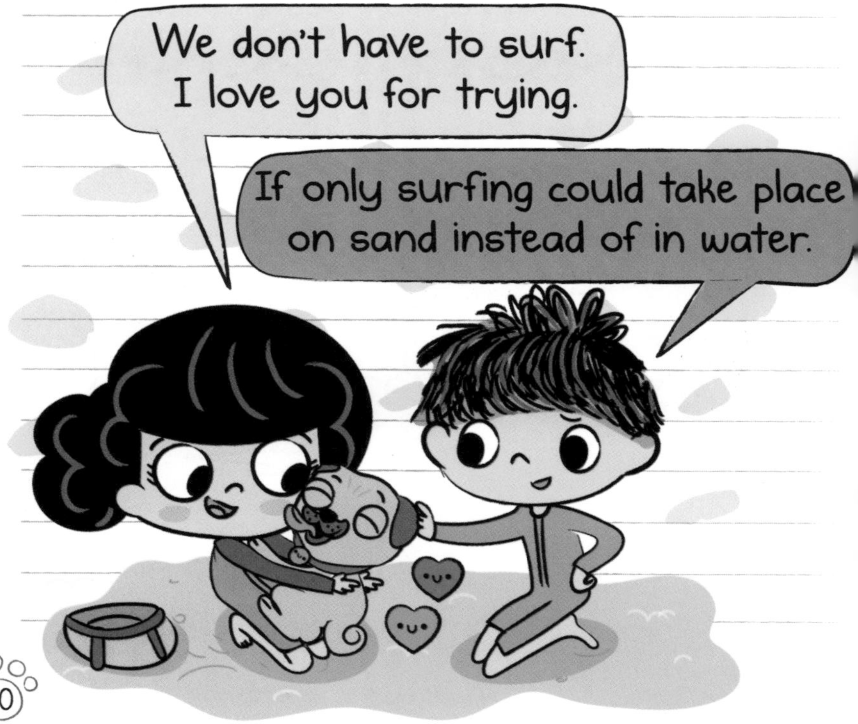
We don't have to surf.
I love you for trying.
If only surfing could take place
on sand instead of in water.

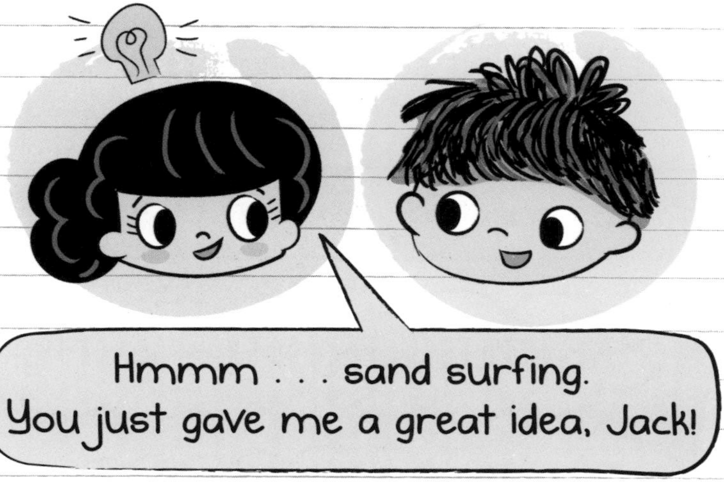
Hmmm . . . sand surfing.
You just gave me a great idea, Jack!

Bella and Jack started digging in the sand . . .

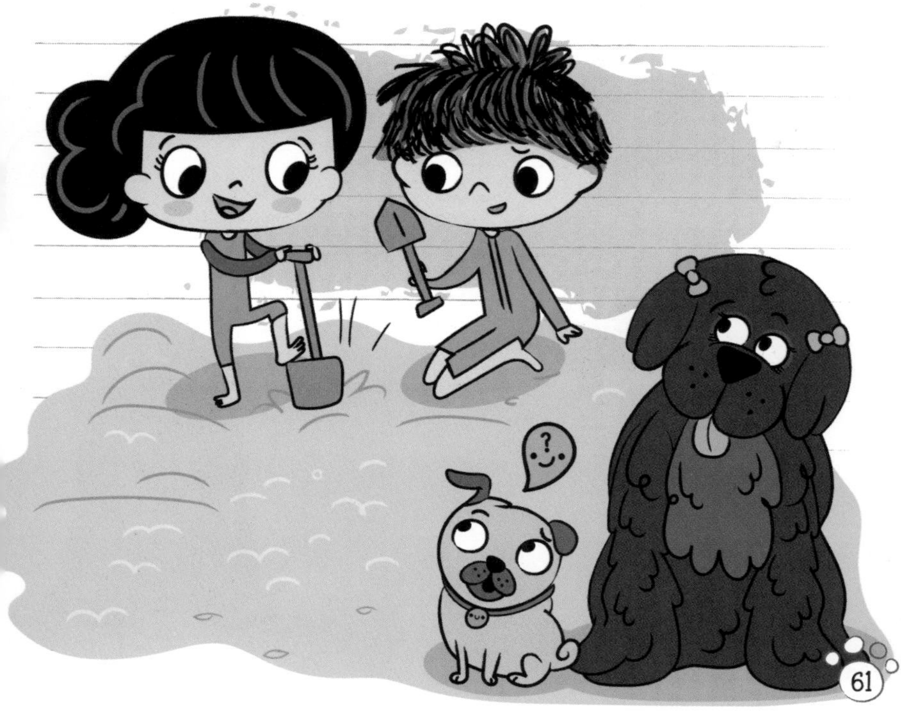
?

And they built something incredible!

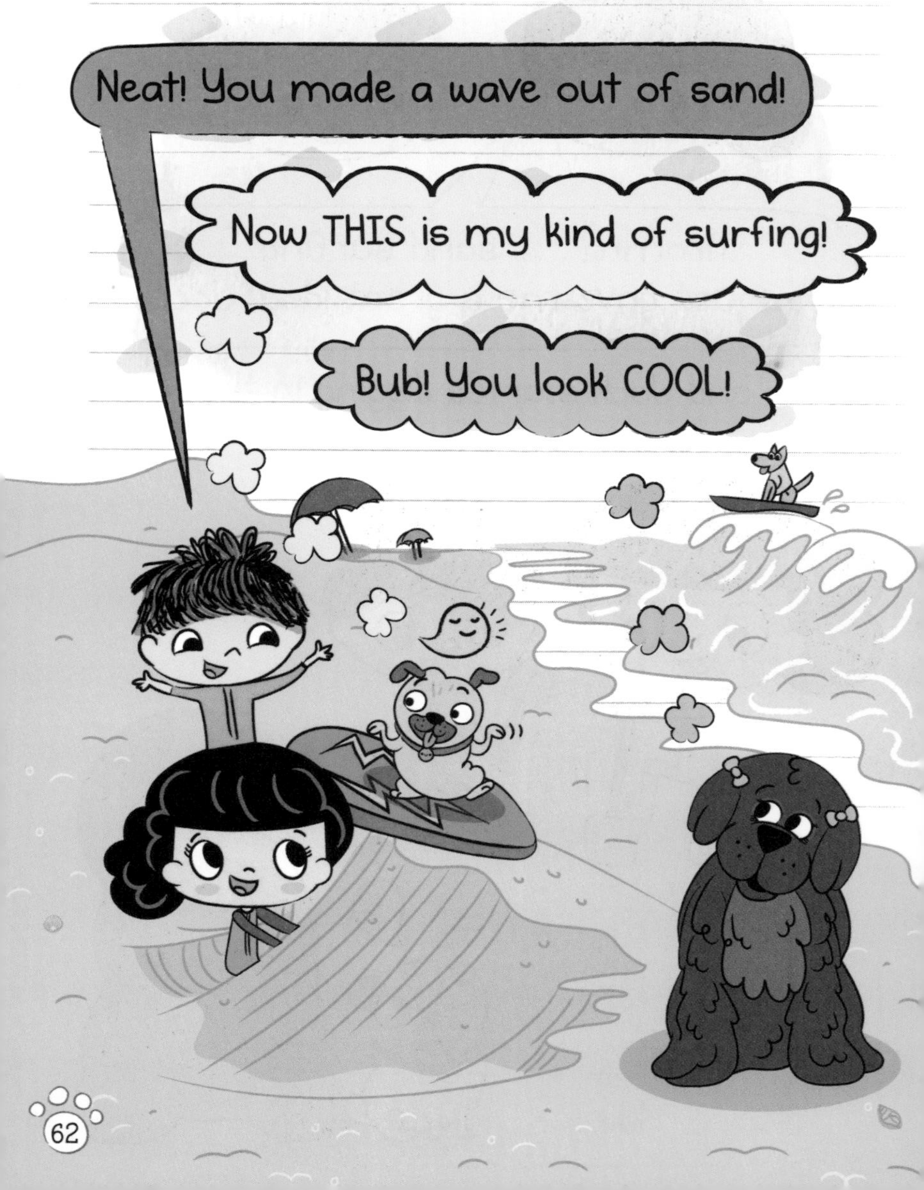
Neat! You made a wave out of sand!
Now THIS is my kind of surfing!
Bub! You look COOL!

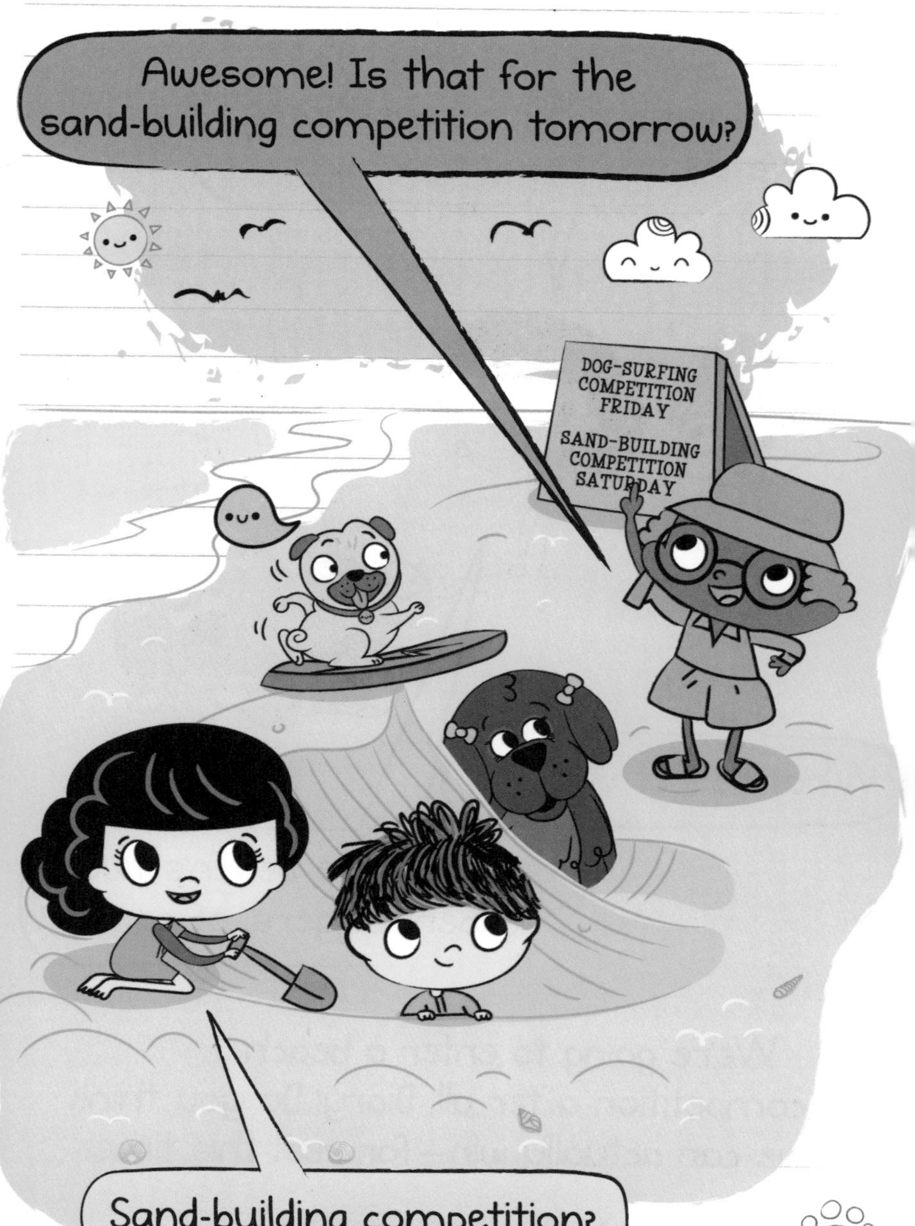
Awesome! Is that for the sand-building competition tomorrow?
DOG-SURFING COMPETITION FRIDAY
SAND-BUILDING COMPETITION SATURDAY
Sand-building competition?

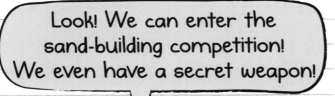

Look! We can enter the sand-building competition! We even have a secret weapon!

DOG-SURFING
COMPETITION
FRIDAY

SAND-BUILDING
COMPETITION
SATURDAY

What secret weapon?

Treasure Beach's two expert diggers, of course!

We're going to enter a beach competition after all, Diary! Do you think we can actually win—for real this time?

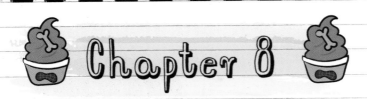

Chapter 8

BUB THE BEACH PUG

SATURDAY

Dear Diary,

Bella got me up bright and early to start building!

We'll need shovels and pails and pup paws!

Bella had drawn up a plan for us to follow. It looked COOLER than cool!

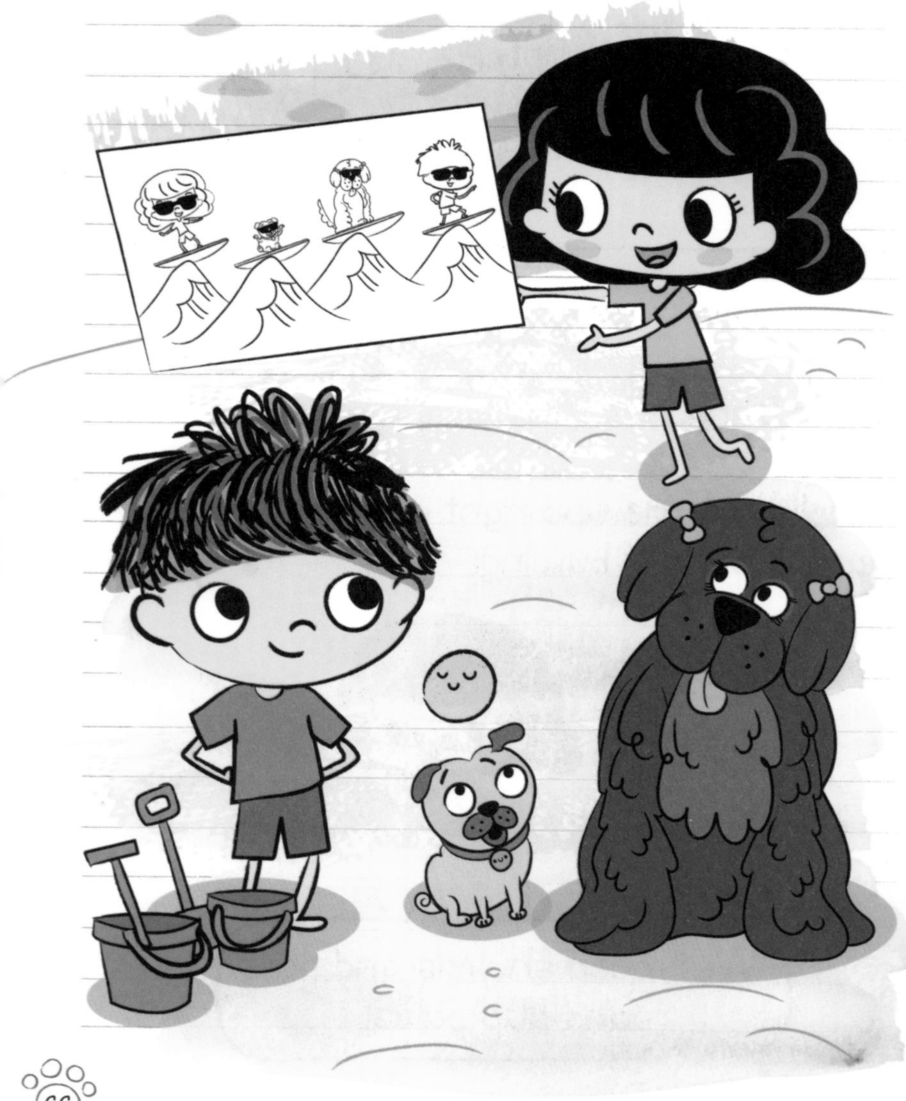

We dug and built and sculpted. Then we dug and built and sculpted some more.

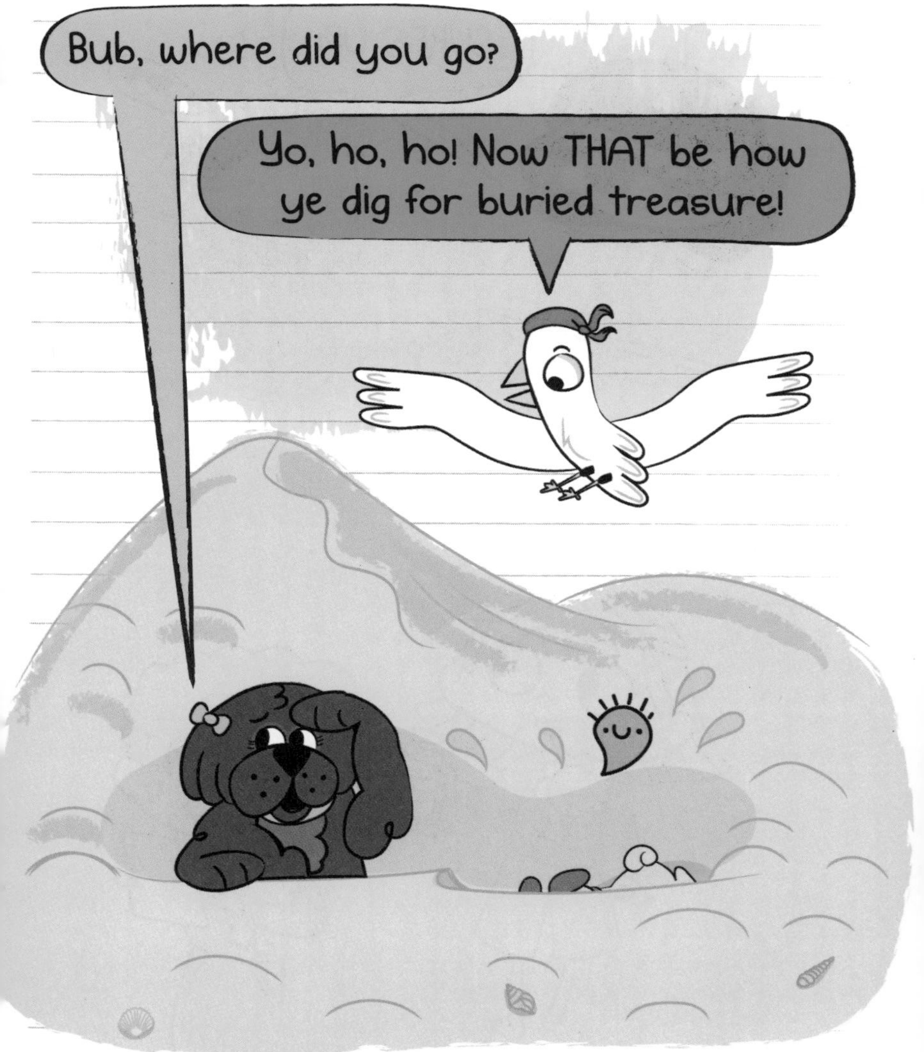
Bub, where did you go?
Yo, ho, ho! Now THAT be how ye dig for buried treasure!

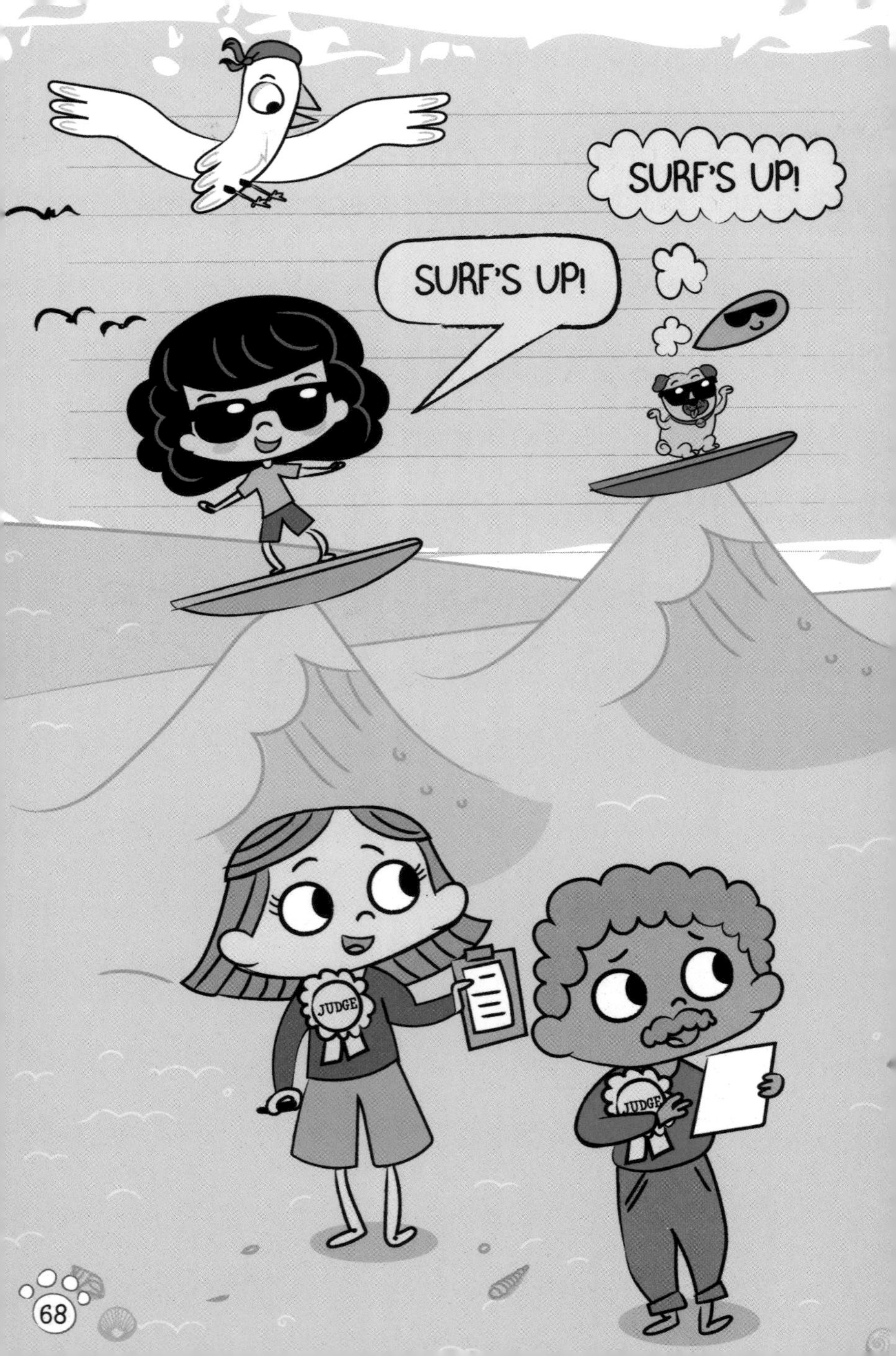
SURF'S UP!
SURF'S UP!
JUDGE
JUDGE

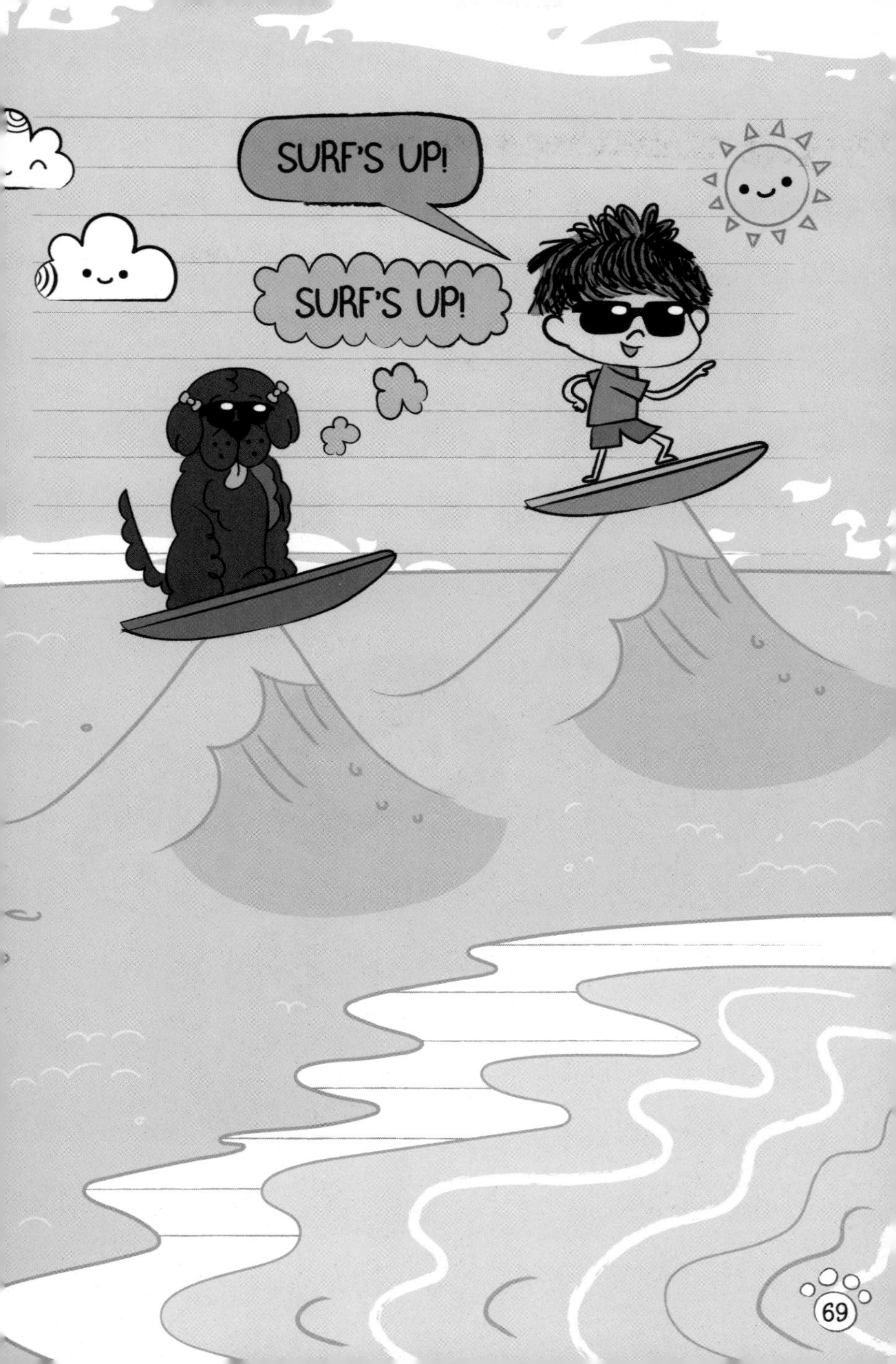
SURF'S UP!
SURF'S UP!

I couldn't believe it, Diary! We won first place!

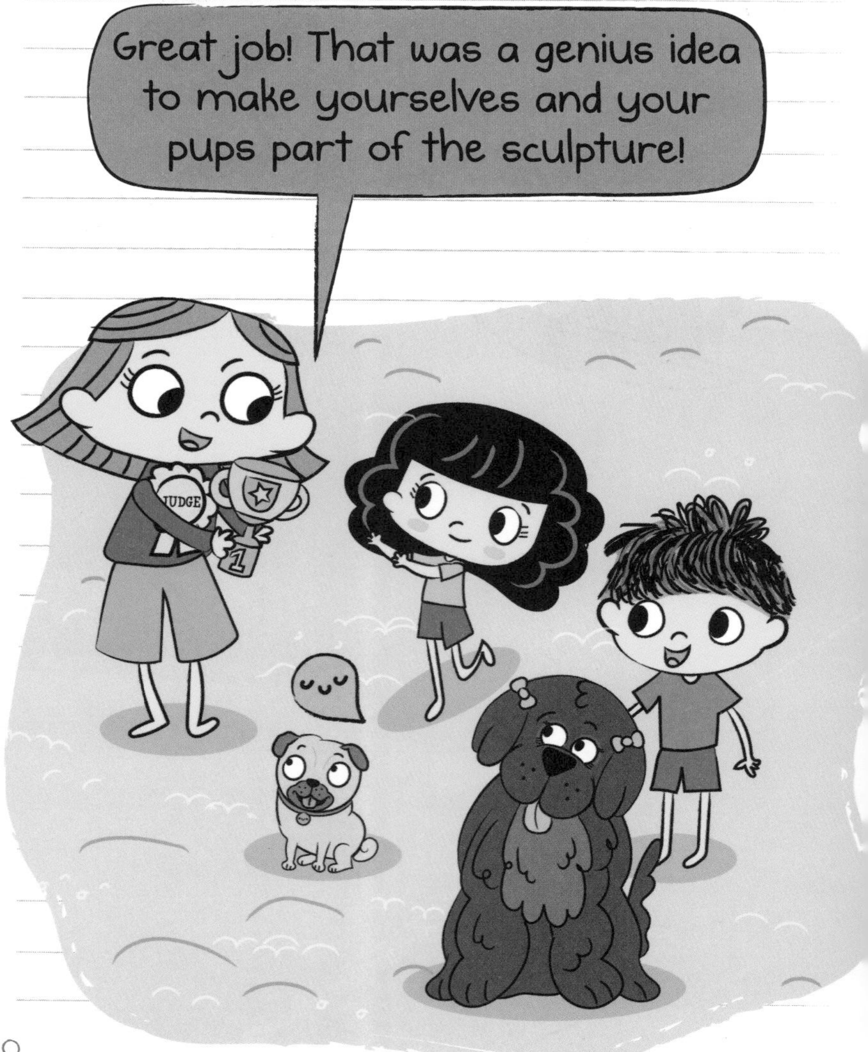
Great job! That was a genius idea to make yourselves and your pups part of the sculpture!
JUDGE
1

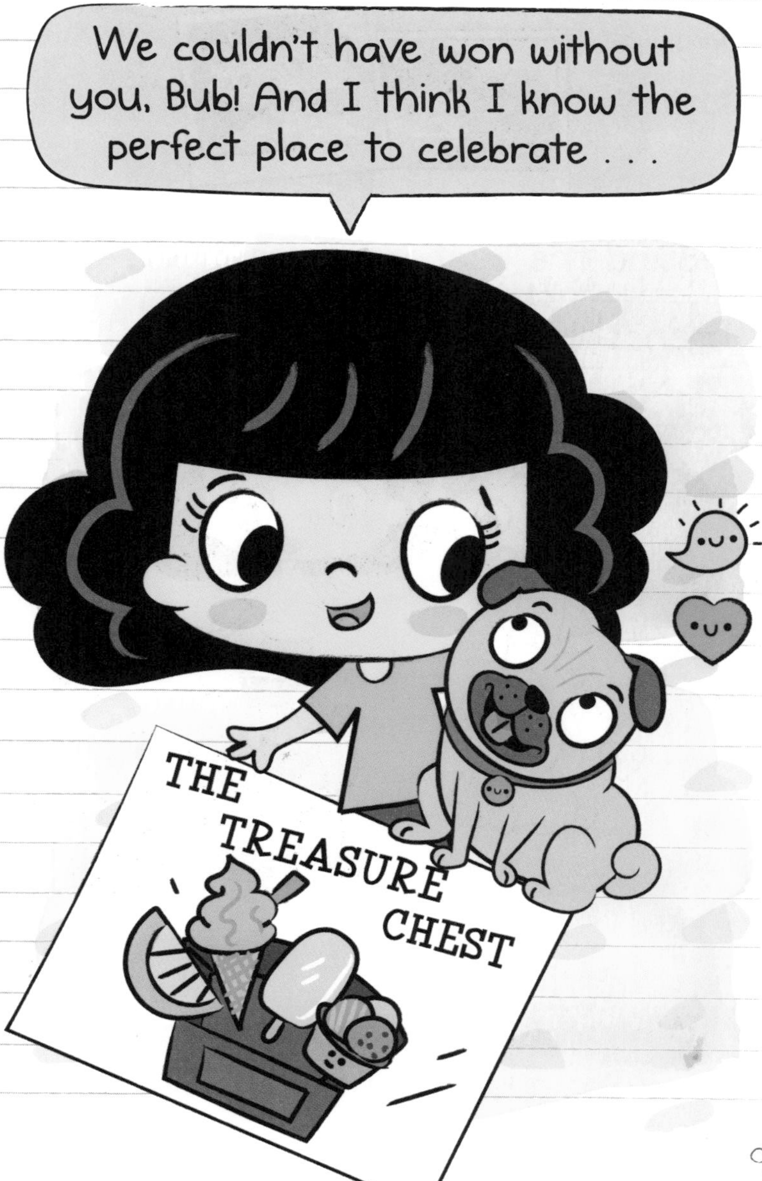
We couldn't have won without you, Bub! And I think I know the perfect place to celebrate . . .
THE TREASURE CHEST

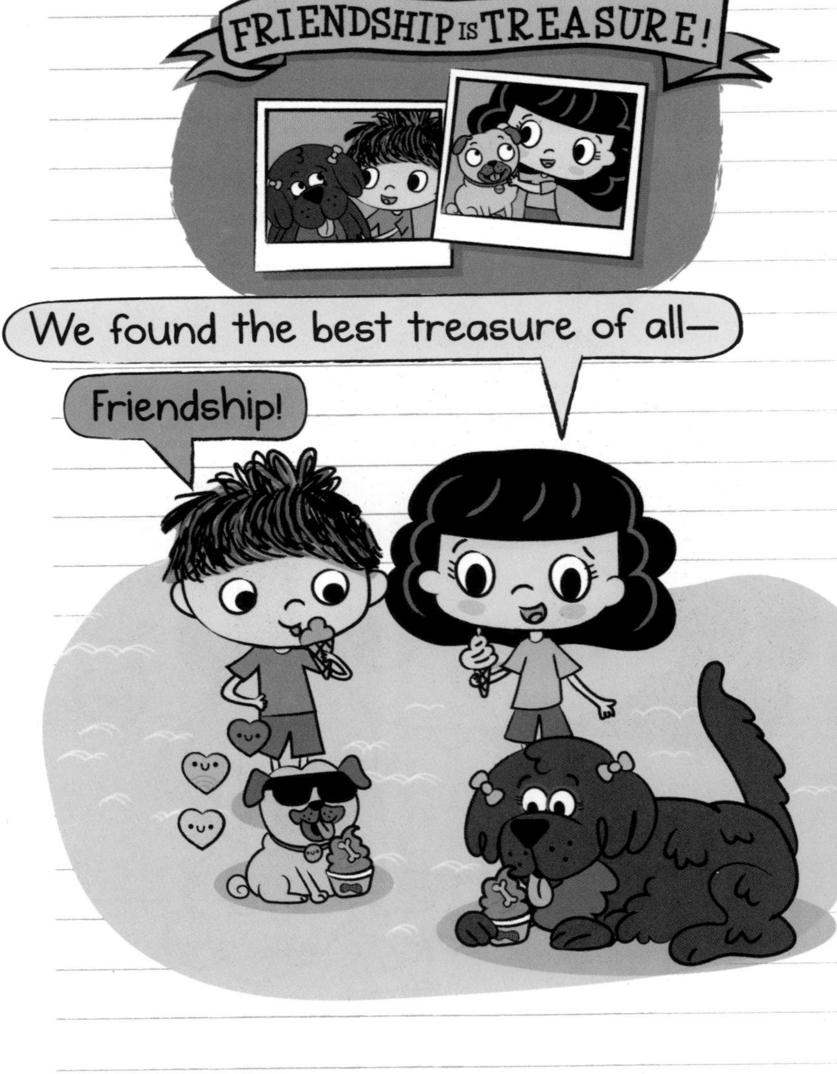
FRIENDSHIP IS TREASURE!
We found the best treasure of all—
Friendship!

Who would have thought, Diary? I guess I'm a beach pug after all!

About the Creator

Kyla May ♥

Kyla May is an Australian illustrator, writer, and designer. In addition to books, Kyla creates animation. She lives by the beach in Victoria, Australia, with her three daughters, two cats, and two dogs. Bub the Pug was inspired by her daughter's pug.

HOW MUCH DO YOU KNOW ABOUT

DIARY OF A PUG

Beach Pug?

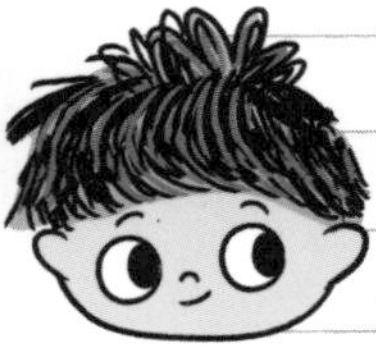

When Bub backs out of the dog-surfing competition, Luna tries surfing instead. Why doesn't it work out? Reread page 16.

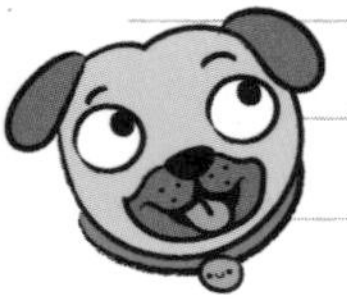

Luna and I visit three places on our treasure hunt. Draw your own treasure map! Include three places or clues leading to the treasure.

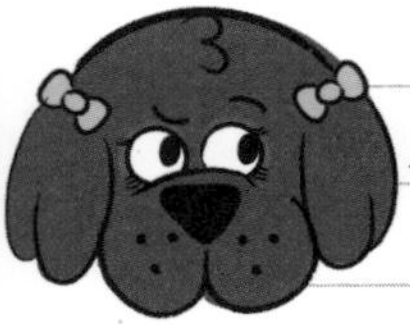

The seagull teaches Bub and me about the tides. What is a tide? Reread page 23.

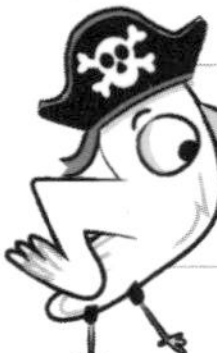

September 19 is International Talk Like a Pirate Day. Try talking like a pirate any day of the year!

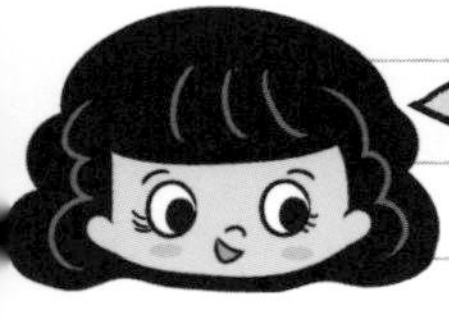

Foreshadowing is a hint about something that will happen later in a story. Is there foreshadowing in this book? Hint: Reread page